To John.
James Barker.

Pioneers of Second Fork

James P. Burke

authorHOUSE®

Contact the author through: jburke@mtzionhistoricalsociety.org
www.mtzionhistoricalsociety.org

AuthorHouse™
1663 Liberty Drive, Suite 200
Bloomington, IN 47403
www.authorhouse.com
Phone: 1-800-839-8640

First published by AuthorHouse 5/7/2009

ISBN: 978-1-4389-4828-7 (sc)
ISBN: 978-1-4389-4829-4 (hc)

Library of Congress Control Number: 2009900591

Printed in the United States of America
Bloomington, Indiana

This book is printed on acid-free paper.

Lynda Pontzer an internationally recognized portrait and landscape artist did the cover painting of Pioneers of Second Fork. As a resident of Elk County, Pontzer has painted numerous landscapes on location and local residents from life. Pontzer's work maybe viewed at www.PortraitAndLandscapes.com

PIONEERS OF SECOND FORK
INTRODUCTION

PIONEERS OF SECOND FORK – Presents an interesting and fascinating history of the early westward marching pioneers who came to settle the headwaters of Susquehanna River at a place known as Second Fork. The family profiles of Second Fork traces this land from Seneca Indian territory to established settlements on the Bennett's Branch. These true-life accounts vividly portray the pioneers' struggles, accomplishments and setbacks in carving out an existence in this once wild perilous land.

The history of these families touches on both the ancestry and descendants of these pioneer settlers from diversified backgrounds and their reasons for coming to this land. For example, Old Andrew, a German immigrant known as a newcomer, indentured himself and his family to come to American to escape religious and political persecution in his quest for freedom. He became one of the very first settlers on the Bennett's Branch. Some settlers came from families of means to seek the opportunities the vast resources this land offered, such as the huge stands of magnificent giant pine trees that once dominated the mountainsides of the valley.

Pioneers of Second Fork is an extensively researched history of 16 adventuresome settlers who endured and overcame many hardships to civilize this beautiful, but once primitive land. From a shoot out on the banks of Sinnemahoning River to the Paul Bunyan of Penn's woods, Second Fork presents many interesting and captivating stories of pioneer life on the Bennett's Branch.

James Burke is a lifelong resident of the Bennett's Valley area. Here is your opportunity to journey with him as he uncovers the past through the lives of these 16 fascinating first settlers of the Second Fork.

Table of Contents

Peter Grove – The Grove Party   7

Hicks   15

The Morey Family   29

The Lewis Family   49

Andreas Oberdoff – Andrew Overturf Family   67

The Dents   81

The Mix Family   97

The Winslows   105

The Weeds   129

The Webb's   135

Noah Kincaid And Family   149

Johnson Family History   161

Anthony Benezet And The History Of Benezett(E)   179

The Den(N)Isons   189

Brookins Family   201

The Bliss Family   211

PETER GROVE – THE GROVE PARTY

During the Revolutionary War, the settlers on Pennsylvania's western frontier were at war with the Seneca Indians and their allies. The British paid the Indians for scalps of colonial settlers, and in turn the colonial government offered a bounty for Indian scalps. The consequence resulted in many money-driven Indian raids on Pennsylvania's western frontier in which countless settlers, including women and children, were killed and/or scalped.

Anthony Grove, in 1756, was a private in Captain Joseph Shippen's Company at Fort Augusta, built in 1756-57, at the confluence of the West and North branches of the Susquehanna River near the present day city of Sunbury, a place the Indians called Shamokin. Fort Augusta was a strategic stronghold in the wilderness for protection of the early settlers then living and migrating up the river during the French and Indian War. The fort later served as a military base

AUGUSTA FORT

Fort Augusta was Pennsylvania's stronghold in the upper Susquehanna Valley from the new days of the French and Indian War to the close of the American Revolution. This site is now within the limits of the City of Sunbury, is an area the Indians called "Shamokin". First constructed as part of the British defense against the raids of the French and Indians from the upper Allegheny region, it was later used as an American fortress: in the protection of the settlers of the upper Susquehanna from Britain's Indian allies to the north. It was named for the mother of King George III.

The picture and script is courtesy of

The Northumberland County

providing refuge for the settlers during Pontiac's Rebellion and the Revolutionary War. In 1780, Anthony's sons would answer their call to duty as Fort Augusta defenders.

What happened in 1780-81 on the banks of Sinnemahoning near the mouth of Grove Run, just a few miles downstream from the mouth of Second Branch, paints a vivid portrait of the events just prior to the arrival of the first pioneer settlers to this bountiful, but perilous wilderness on the Bennett's Branch.

THE DEADLY INDIAN RAID

The Indians raided a settlement in the general vicinity of Fort Augusta and killed a number of settlers including a man named Klinesmith, a personal friend of Peter Grove. In addition to this deadly raid, according to Lt. Moses Van Campen's written deposition submitted with his petition to Congress for a pension, in the summer of 1781 a man came into the fort claiming to have escaped from his Indian captors. He reported that there were approximately 300 Indians camped on Sinnemahoning preparing for an all out attack on the settlers living on Pennsylvania's western frontier. He further reported that the Indians planned to divide into small units and to unify their attack by striking on the same day. Colonel Samuel Hunter, in response to this distressing news, quickly organized a party of experienced scouts to reconnoiter the Sinnemahoning regarding movements of the Indians.

Almost immediately following the massacre, a quick decision was made to pursue the Indians in retaliation of their deadly raid. The Grove party, comprised of Peter and Michael Grove, Jacob Creamer, and William Campbell prepared for their excursion into hostile Indian country by disguising themselves as Indians, darkening their skin and dressing in Indian garb. Outfitted with three weeks provisions and with a war-whoop, they started on their mission up the Susquehanna River on the trail of the Indian war party. That evening they stopped at James Ellis's house near

Fort Muncy where they anxiously ate dinner with their muskets on their knees while maintaining a constant vigil for danger.

On the afternoon of the third day, near the mouth of Young Woman Creek, the party discovered a camp of about twenty-five or thirty Indians. The Indians did not have a fire that evening, evidently fearful of pursuit. The Grove Party, considerably outnumbered, decided to keep a careful watch on the Indian party in an effort to determine their movements and overall strengths.

The next morning the Indians broke camp and proceeded at a rather fast pace up the river. The Grove party followed but kept to the hillsides to avoid being discovered. When the party reached Cooks Run, just a few miles above the current town of Renovo, they decided to follow an Indian trail which led over the mountain to the head waters of Ellicott Run and then down a trail alongside the run to where the run empties into First Fork. This point is just a short distance upstream from the mouth of First Fork. Here it appears that the Indians divided into two groups, one continuing on up the Sinnemahoning while the second group proceeded up First Fork.

ON THEIR TRAIL

The Grove party crossed First Fork and proceeded to the top of the mountain overlooking the present town of Sinnemahoning. It was late in the day and upon reaching the top of the mountain the party could smell smoke from a campfire. Feeling confident that this was smoke coming from an Indian campsite, the party cautiously made their way down the mountain side towards the smoke.

Near the foot of the mountain they found some bushes to conceal themselves from the Indians. Here they silently waited for an opportunity to attack. As darkness began to prevail over the valley, Peter Grove crept in towards the Indian camp to assess the situation while the other members of the party primed their muskets and sharpened their flints in preparation for a fight.

Peter observed that there were about twelve Indians camped near the mouth of a small stream that formed a large pool of water just before entering the main branch. Near the mouth of the small stream next to the river's edge stood a large oak tree. A large limb, at least eighteen inches in diameter, protruded from the main trunk of the tree on the side next to the river opposite the small stream. The limb ran out twelve or fifteen feet, drooping towards the ground. The Indians in preparing to make camp for the night, built a small punky fire, struck their hatchets into the limb of the big tree, and leaned their muskets against the trunk of the tree. Peter intently watched as the Indians began to lie down and wrap themselves in their bedrolls.

Peter sneaked quietly back to where the other members of the party had concealed themselves and made them aware of the situation. Although considerably outnumbered, they had the advantage of surprise. The four men silently crawled with a hatchet in one hand and a musket in the other towards the light of the campfire. When they approached within a very short distance of the campfire, an old Indian woke up with a severe cough, and as he was coughing, he appeared to be staring directly at them as sensing danger.

The few minutes it took for the old Indian to return to his bed roll and fall back to sleep seemed like an eternity .The men patiently waited. Anxiety for revenge intensified with each passing moment. Finally the old Indian laid back down, apparently falling back to sleep. As they renewed their cautious crawl toward the fire and the sleeping Indians, one of Grove's scouts unexpectedly bumped into one of the Indians lying further back from the fire than the other Indians. At the same moment the old Indian arose in alarm.

Suddenly the valley erupted with death defying war whoops as the Grove Party ferociously charged the Indians. Michael Grove, with a powerful thrust of his hatchet, drove it into the skull of the old Indian, and then turned and buried his hatchet into the back of a second Indian. Unable to withdraw his hatchet, Michael and the Indian tumbled down over the bank as the other scouts were swinging their hatchets with a violent and deadly fury. The sleeping Indians began rising from the ground like a dark cloud, dazed and bewildered, to the roar and smoke of the Grove Party firing their muskets. The surviving Indians, apparently feeling they were being attacked by a much larger force, plunged into the Main Branch, and escaped under the cover of darkness, wading to the far bank of the river. As Michael climbed up over the small bank with a scalp in his hand, the others were breaking the locks on the remaining Indians muskets and throwing them into the pond. Eight or nine Indians lay dead near the base of the oak tree.

The Hunted Hunters

Time was now of extreme essence. If the Grove party was to survive this skirmish they would have to make a hasty retreat. It wouldn't take long for the Indians to realize the size of the small attacking party. The hunters had now become the hunted. Fortunately Michael Grove was blessed with eyes like a night hawk. He could travel nearly as fast at night as he could by day. Grove swiftly guided the party twelve miles down along the river's shore line to where the Sinnemahoning enters the Susquehanna River.

Just below the confluence of the two rivers, the Grove Party left visible footprints on a sand bar to mislead the Indians. They then waded the river and back-tracked up the river a short distance. Here they left the river on the south side where the bluffs come down to the water's edge and climbed the mountainside to make their way to Bald Eagle Creek. When they reached the top of Bald Eagle mountain they looked down in the valley below and could see about twenty-five Indians apparently in pursuit on the north side of the river just a short distance above Lock Haven. The undetected party proceeded along the summit of the mountain, following a trail which led through Nippenose Valley and on to safety in Buffalo Valley.

The Grove Party

According to Van Campen's deposition, this party, known as the Grove Party, consisted of Captain Campbell, Peter and Michael Grove, Lt. Cramer, and Van Campen himself as leader. However, the "History of the West Branch Valley" relates this incident as "after the murder of Klinesmith [a friend of the Grove Family] Captain Peter Grove, his brother Michael Grove, Lieutenant Cramer and William Campbell resolved to pursue the Indians and not return until they secured a few scalps." (Page 661) This account does not mention Lt. Moses Van Campen.

The State Treasurer's account, dated September 30, 1780, indicates they paid Jacob Creamer, Peter and Michael Grove and William Campbell for two Indian scalps.

Beers reports in the History of McKean, Elk, Cameron and Potter Counties, in context, that in 1839 William Floyd went down the river to Shamokin, and on over to Buffalo Valley where he visited with Peter Grove just two years prior the pioneer's death. In 1842 Floyd related the story to Francis J. Chadwick who published the Grove Story in the columns of the Press in 1878. It appears from this account that after the massacre, the two Groves along with a friend resolved to revenge the killings of their comrades and to pursue the Indians to the Sinnemahoning.

The "Annals of Buffalo Valley" states "He {Michael Grove} told Beeber that Joseph Groninger, of White Deer, was along. {Member of the Grove Party}

The available evidence would strongly suggest that the Grove Party consisted of the four scouts indicated above, which did not include Van Campen and an Indian guide. The incident occurred in 1780, instead of 1781 as indicated in Van Campen's deposition.

Shorty before the end of the eighteenth century, Pennsylvania acquired title to the territory west of the Alleganies from the Iroquois Indians in an agreement known as the "1784-5 Last Purchase."

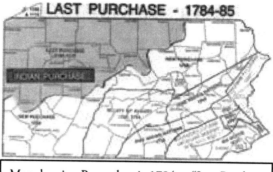

Map showing Pennsylvania 1784 – "Last Purchase
Courtesy of Commonwealth of Pennsylvania

The Holland Land Co., in a series of lengthy and complicated negotiations, acquired title to large tracts of land in this purchase which included most of what we know today as Elk, Cameron and McKean Counties. In the early eighteen hundreds, the Holland Land Company offered this land for sale to the westward-marching pioneer settlers.

The pathway to Second Fork is located in the headwaters of the Susquehanna River. Before the days of roads the rivers served as the major highways for the early settlers seeking to purchase these newly available lands. These intrepid pioneers would canoe upstream on the Sinnemahoning until they came to the confluence of Second Fork, now known as the Bennett's Branch. Just before arriving at Second Fork, about two miles above First Fork, where the village of Sinnemahoning is now located, these settlers would encounter a small stream entering the Sinnemahoning from the north side. Standing prominently on the edge of the river's bank, near the mouth of this small stream, stood the large, majestic white oak tree, a silent witness to the passage of time.

THE LAND MARK

The stream in Sinnemahoning is named in honor of Peter and Michael Grove – Grove Run. The scars inflicted by the Indian hatchets on the White Oak tree remained until 1847, and for many years served as a landmark for the pioneers coming up the Sinnemahoning and on to the Bennett's Branch to settle. William Nelson stated when his father moved to the Sinnemahoning, he visited the battle ground in 1842, and counted twelve distinct marks of tomahawks in the bark of the big limb. This ancient oak, with a girth exceeding 30 inches and its lowest branch more than 24 feet from the ground, stood solid as a visible landmark for the Indians and the settlers. Time and nature was about to undue this majestic sentinel. The Great Flood of October 8, 1847 undermined the roots of this giant eventually causing the tree to rot. The flood of 1861 dealt the final death knell as the great White Oak washed away, leaving just a few minor artifacts and a grand memory of our forefathers' struggles to tame and settle these lands.

THE END

History of McKean, Elk, Cameron and Potter Counties, Penn – Beers
History of Lebanon County – Grove Brothers' Homestead
1875 Atlas of Lebanon County,
Northumberland County Historical Society
Sunbury Gazette and Miner's Register, dated November 17, 1838
History of the West Branch.
Annals of Buffalo Valley, Pennsylvania by John Blair Linn.

HICKS

HICKS RUN! Named after Gershom Hicks, a colorful character who lived in a perilous time when a man's life depended upon his ability to survive. Captured by Indians when he was just a boy, Gershom

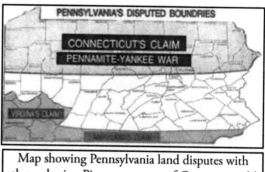

Map showing Pennsylvania land disputes with other colonies Picture courtesy of Commonwealth of Pennsylvania Dept. of Internal Affairs.

lived with them the better part of his life. When he grew into manhood, Gershom was an Indian trader with a questionable reputation in the Ohio Valley. During the French and Indian War, the English General Gage wanted Hicks captured and hung as a traitor. Escaping execution for the lack of evidence, Gershom went on to fight as a continental soldier in the Revolutionary War. In 1790, following the war, Gershom signed on as guide to help Samuel MaClay survey the streams and waterways in Pennsylvania's "Last Purchase." Sometime later, about 1812, Levi Hicks settled near the mouth of Hicks Run. Many historians and Hicks family genealogists are firmly convinced, but can not document that Gershom was Levi's uncle. Levi has the distinction of floating the first long raft down the Bennett's Branch.

Gershom Hicks was born about 1734, when there was much conflict and turmoil for control of lands in what is now Pennsylvania. The western part of Pennsylvania was Seneca Indian Territory; the French claimed all the lands in the Mississippi watershed which included a sizable portion of Pennsylvania, extending into what is now Elk County. The English Colony of Pennsylvania claimed all the land extending 5 degrees latitude west of the Delaware River, which extended into the Ohio Valley. This boundary was set forth and described in King Charles II's charter granted to William Penn, dated March 4, 1681. In addition to this power struggle among the Indians, France, England, and the settlers, Pennsylvania had a number of border disputes with the other colonies. Virginia claimed the southwestern portion of what now is Pennsylvania in and around the confluence of the Allegheny and Monongahela Rivers forming the Ohio River. This was the site of Fort Pitt, present day site of downtown Pittsburgh. There was a dispute with Maryland regarding Pennsylvania's southern border, while Connecticut claimed the northern portion of Pennsylvania, including all of what is now Elk County. It would take many bloody encounters with the Indians, two wars - The French and Indian and The Revolutionary Wars - together with numerous negotiations for Pennsylvania to evolve into it present state. Gershom Hicks lived in these times, and played a role in this evolution.

Gershom and his two brothers, Mosses and Levi, were captured by the Indians when they were very young boys. By the time Gershom was thirty, he had spent the greater part of his life living with the Indians.

Up to the start of the French and Indian War, about 1763, Gershom was an Indian fur trader in the upper Ohio Valley. A trader's life had many adventuresome moments, death-defying encounters, and unbelievable hardships, but all in all a very profitable profession if you could survive wilderness life. Stephen Brule, the first known trader to set foot in Pennsylvania, was eaten by the Indians. He came to America in 1608 with the famous French explorer Champlain.

Indian fur traders played a very important role as explorers and pathfinders into the wilderness on Pennsylvania's western frontier. The traders were the sole source of supplies for European manufactured goods such as guns, powder, metal cookware, beads and other items upon which the Indians had become desperately dependent. As a result of their trading activities they became the main link between the Indians in the Ohio Valley and the westward marching settlers.

Indian fur traders in the Ohio Valley during the first half of the 1700s, had a notorious reputation for their evil behavior. Ben Franklin described Indian Traders as "The most vicious and abandoned wretches of our nation." Although there were a number of honest traders such as Hugh Crawford, George Croghan, Christopher Gist and George Morgan, to mention a few, who treated the Indians honestly and maintained a peaceable relationship, there were a number of other traders with a history of wicked and despicable behavior that included but was not limited to such immoral acts as murder, rape and arson, as well as lying and cheating the Indians out of their furs.. The actions of this disgraceful lot of characters considerably outweighed the efforts of the honest traders and caused a number of serious problems and conflicts between the Indians and settlers. Trading rum to the Indians was against the law, but neither the British nor the Colonial governments could enforce this law, as the trading activities were too far removed from civilization. Traders would often get the Indians drunk on potent rum and then trade watered down rum for their goods. Even some of the honest traders would give the Indians spirits. Louis Long, father of the famous hunter Bill Long, who established a trading post in the Du Bois Area, often gave the Indians whiskey. His trading post was known by many local Seneca Indians as a still house where they would often go for drunken orgies. Before Long would give the Indians whiskey, he would lock their guns, knives and tomahawks in a strong box, and return them only after they had sobered up. Long treated the Indians fairly and enjoyed a friendly relationship with them. His son Bill had a number of Indian friends and learned many hunting skills from them.

Gersham Hicks, along with fellow traders such as Joseph Campbell, the Girty Brothers, James Duning, Matthew Elliot, Hugh Parker, John Powle, Peter Shaver, and John Young, was considered among the latter group of dishonest and despicable traders.

The following article was published in 1766, as a public plea for the cause of the American Indians. The author endeavors to describe the shameful practices of traders, and portray the typical attitude of these contemptible individuals. M'Dole, plays the role as trader who cheats the Indians for a profit regardless of the consequences, while Murphy is a newcomer learning the art of being a successful Indian trader.

M'Dole, "Tis very well; your Articles are good; but now the Thing's to make a Profit from them, worth all your toil and Pains of coming hither. Our fundamental Maximum then is this, that it's no Crime to cheat and gull an Indian."

Murphy, "How! Not a Sin to cheat an Indian, say you? Are they not Men? Haven't they a Right to Justice As well as we, though savage in their Manners?"

M'Dole, "Ah! If you boggle here, I say no more;; This is the very Quintessence of Trade, And ev'ry Hope of Gin depends upon it. None who neglect it ever did grow rich, Or ever will, or can by Indian Commerce. By this Ogden built his stately House, purchas'd Estates, and grew a little King. He, like an honest Man bought all by Weight, and made the ignorant Savages believe That his Right Foot exactly weigh'd a Pound: By this for many Years he bought their Furs And died in Quiet like an honest Dealer."

Murphey, "Well, I'll not stick at what is necessary, But his Device is now grown old and stale, Not could I manage such a barefa'd Fraud."

M'Dole, "A thousand Opportunities present To take Advantage of their ignorance, But the great Engine I employ is Rum, More powerful made by certain strengthening Drugs. This I distribute with a lib'ral Hand. Urge them to drink till they grow mad and valiant; Which makes them think me generous and just, And gives full Scope to practice all my Art. I then begin my trade with water'd Rum, the cooling Draught well suits their scorching Throats. Their Fur and Peltry come in quick Return. My Scales are honest, but so well contrived, That one small Slip will turn Three

General Thomas Gage
Courtesy of
COMMONWEALTH OF
MASSACHUSETTS
ART COMMISSION

Pounds to One, Which they, poor silly Souls! Ignorant of Weights And Rules of Balancing, do not perceive."

In 1763, the Indians went on a rampage, declaring war on the English and settlers on the Western frontier, burning and attacking forts in the Ohio Valley, including Fort Erie, Fort Le Bouef, Fort Venago (Franklin), Fort Pitt, and Fort Detroit. The following year the English, together with militias of American colonies, marched on the Indians to squelch their threat and regain control of this area. General Gage took his army on the northern route along the lakes, while Col. Bouquet marched his troops in the South using Fort Pitt as his base. During this campaign General Gage received reports that Gershom Hicks had participated in raids with the Indians against several of the settlements. Gage wanted to capture Hicks and hang him as a spy. While the correspondence was going back and forth between General Gage and Colonel Bouquet concerning Gershom, Gershom arrived at Fort Pitt, claiming to have escaped from the Indians. The following is Gershom Hicks' deposition which was given to Captain Grant, commanding Fort Pitt at this time.

Date April 14, 1764,

DEPOSITION OF GERSHOM
(GORSHAM) HICKS!

Gershom Hicks a man about Thirty years of age, arrived at Fort Pitt having made his escape from the Indians, says that he was a Servant to Patrick Allison, an Indian Trader, and was made Prisoner last May, by the Shawnees, near Muskingum, the rest of his fellow Horse Drivers (four in number) being killed by the savages, about the same time, the Shawnees kept him prisoner about four days, then gave him to a Delaware, known by the name of Captain Bullet, who kept him near twenty days at a place called Moquesin, a Delaware Town on Muskingum River: from thence he was sent to help to build a House at the Salt Licks, for White Eyes, a Delaware Chief, at which place he remained all winter hunting thereabouts for meat, for himself and some other White Prisoners that were with the Delaware's at that place, (vis John Gibson & one Morris) that about thirty days ago he was sent to a place called Hockhocbin, where King Beaver lives at present about Thirty Miles on this side of Scioto, There he was to hunt in company with two Delaware's, that in a few days one of them left him & went home again to go to war, leaving orders with Hicks to follow him which he did do in eight or nine days afterwards and went up the Hockhocking River for near a mile leaving the other Indian by himself to hunt . He thought this a good time to come off, so turned back again with his Canoe & came into the Ohio River, into which the Hochocking River empties itself, then crossed the Ohio to the South East Side when he left his Canoe and came up by Land having his Gun and about Twenty Loads of Powder and Ball with him. Says this is eight days ago and that he saw three Indians the day before yesterday making a Raft to cross the River, to the side he was on about 100 miles below the Fort, He further says that there was a Council held at the Salt Licks, last fall by the Delaware's in which it was agreed that two of their Chiefs with White Eyes should be sent to some of the French Forts on the Mississippi, who accordingly went to ask the French to join them to make ware against the English this Spring and to give them some Ammunition, which Articles he says he is very sure neither the Shawnees or Delaware's have above a pint and many of them but half a pint of Powder each man and lead in

Proportion.(N.B. Hicks speaks the Delaware language very well also understands the Shawnees Tongue a little and as the Indians had great confidence in him from his being a Prisoner with them once before, and having what he calls Friends among them he was therefore trusted with all their Secrets and Designs) further says that White Eyes and the two other Chiefs returned again the beginning of last March very much dissatisfied with the answers they got from the French and that they were not provided ammunition at all except three pints, and a little powder to carry them home again, telling them to go back and take care of their wives and children that they were all as one with the English now and would not fight against them.

Hicks says he thinks that with the Delaware's and Shawnees he has seen about 50 or 60 * white Prisoners, (sic) and of which one woman and young persons, and most of them taken last war. That the small pox has been very general & raging among the Indians since last Spring and that 30 or 40 Mingoes, as many Delaware's & some Shawnees, died all of the small pox since that time, that it still continues amongst them. He says the general talk amongst the Indians, was that they intended going in

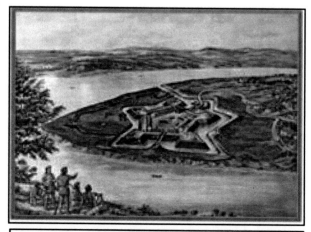

An artist's rendition of Fort Pitt as it appeared around 1776. Picture courtesy of the Pennsylvania State Archives.

large parties this Summer to murder the Frontier Inhabitants, but did not mean to attack any of the Forts, that the Indians are all in want of all kinds of clothing and are obliged to wear skins &c. with regards to Fort Detroit, he says he does not know what is doing there, but that 30 or 50 Ottawa's and Wiandotts were expected by the Delaware's every day to Council, and that he has heard and believes it is the intention to the Delaware's to let the Ottawa's and Wiandotts know that it does not suit them to continue the war, and that as they begun it they must fight it out themselves. He further says that he is very certain the Delaware's have not living above 150 fighting men, and 30 or 40 boys, which is all they can send to war, leaving at the same time about 30 or 40 old men & hunters to take care of their Families & Planting, that the Shawnees, he is not so well acquainted with, but is very sure they have not more than 200 warriors. The Mingoes are very few not above Twenty remaining in that part of the Country, further says that the Shawnees & Delaware's were very uneasy & afraid of the Six Nations Indians Coming to war against them this summer.

Being asked if he heard anything of French Andrew or Aaron, and the Wiandott Indians that went express from this Post to Detroit, says he heard nothing of them & that if they had been detained by any nation on this side of Detroit, he must have heard of it, that the Indians are a little divided amongst themselves about continuing the war, & that King Beaver and Castologa have advised them to Peace, and are still doing the same, and that King Shingoes died last winter further says, that they expect the English will march an army into their Country this Summer, and are much at a loss what to do with their families, having very little Indian Corn for planting and no meat laid up in Store, only what they kill daily and use from hand to mouth.

WILLILAM GRANT
Capt 42 Regiment

Endorsed Deposition of Gorshom Hicks, 14 April 1764

Colonel Henry Bouquet
Painting by John Wollaston

* A case has been made that Lord Jeffrey Amherst, commanding general of British forces in North America at this time, conspired with Colonel Bouquet to give the Indians blankets infected with small pox as a form of germ warfare. Gershom's deposition is considered as evidence to support his claim.

General Gage and Col Bouquet had various correspondences regarding on how to deal with the Hicks brothers. The following are various communications, which remain on record today, between the General and the Colonel concerning Gershom Hicks and his brother Levi.

Date May 2, 1764 - Carlisle
BOUQUET TO GAGE

In part as it relates to Gershom Hicks
"I enclose you a letter from Capt. Grant* as it covers the Deposition of one Hicks I must observe to you that he had lived Voluntarily Several Years with the Indians joined them in their Depredations against us, And that I have the Strongest Reason to believe him a Spy, I desired Capt. Grant to keep him confined if my letter does not come too late-,"

Date May 14, 17640
GAGE TO BOUQUET

In part as it relates to Gershom Hicks
"I have read the Depositions of Hicks, the last has been in Part confirmed by a Trader whom I have examined; who was at Fort Charles Prisoner, when White Eyes and the other two Indians arrived there. Hick is a great villain, I am glad he is secured, and I must desire you will have him tried by a General Court Martial for a spy. Let the Proceedings of the Court prove him a spy as strong as they can. And if He does turn out a spy He must be hanged."

Date October 15, 1764
BOUQUET TO GAGE

In part as it related to Gershom Hicks
"I wish the evidence against Hicks was little more plain, there is nothing to prove him a spy but his own confession, extorted from him

by Threats of Death. I can't therefore confirm the Sentence. Both He and his Brother have been in arms, and you will endeavor to get what proof you can of this that they may be tried Traitors to their Country. But these Trials must be in the country below by the Civil Magistrates to whom they should be given up. The Military may hang a Spy in time of war but the Rebels in Arms are tried by the Civil law at least I saw this practiced in Scotland both by General Hawley & the Duke of Cumberland.

Date November 29, 1764

BOUQUET TO GAGE

In part as it related to Gershom Hicks

"P. S. The two Hicks will be delivered to Mr. Penn's order, to be tried by the Civil Law;"

Rev. Charles Beatty, a minister in Pennsylvania, who ministered in the Ohio Valley, records in his journal: "that on August 21, 1768, after a sermon we rode eight miles to Caption Patterson's where we were kindly received. Here we met with one Levi Hicks, who had been captive of the Indians from his youth, and we being desirous to know their present situation and circumstance gave us the following relation, that about one hundred miles westward of Fort Pitt was an Indian town called Tuskalawas, and at some considerable distance from that was another town name Kighalan????." On August 25, 1768, Rev Beatty records : "Sat out from Captain Patterson's this morning, as early as we could on our journey, accompanied with Joseph, the interpreter, and Levi Hicks. I understood he was considerably impressed under the word of God yesterday, and therefore was desirous to have more sermons."

Gershom Hicks served in the active line of duty as a private in the 1st Regiment from August 1, 1780 to January 1, 1783, then from this date to November 3, 1883, in the 20 Pa   Regiment of the Pennsylvania Militia during the Revolutionary War. Because the Commonwealth was cash poor as a result of the war, but land rich, many Revolutionary War veterans were paid in land. The question here presented is, did Gershom Hicks purchase land with the payment voucher he received on March 9 and May 2, 1785, for his military services, and if so, where was this land.

Sometime about 1784-5 Pennsylvania acquired all the land west of the Alleganies from the Seneca Indians as a result of the Treaties of Fort Stanwick and Big Tree. Pennsylvania desired to develop a plan to build roads between the head waters of the West Branch of the Susquehanna and the Allegheny River. In 1790, Sam Mc Clay was one of three commissioned by the Supreme Executive Council of Pennsylvania to survey the water ways in this wildness land. Gershom Hicks signed on as guide and hand to this surveying party. Mc Clay claimed that Gershom was half Indian and Gershom once had settled at the mouth of Hicks Run. In May of 1790, the Surveying party spent a good deal of time on the Second Fork, later renamed Bennett's Branch after John Bennett, one of the very first settlers in the Bennett's Valley. They noted that Bennett had a cabin at the mouth of Trout Run which appeared to be old. About a month later, during the survey, the party had a peaceable pow-wow with Chief Cornplanter which took place on the Allegany River. Cornplanter had a lodge (village) named Tiozinosongoehto which was located in Potter County near the McKean County line.

Gershom's brother Levi lived in Huntingdon County, near the mouth of Spruce Creek during the Revolutionary War. This land was warranted June 4, 1762, but was not patented until many years later. Sometime during the Colonial period the Bebault brothers erected a simple mill there and made some other minor improvements on the left side of the Creek. In 1778, Levi and his wife, who was half-Indian, lived there and ran the mill. Levi's brothers, Mosses and Gershom, both unmarried, had a home on nearby Water Street which borders Spruce Creek.

During the Revolutionary War, Indian raids in this part of the country were a common occurrence. Most of the settlements in this part of the country had forts for refuge during these attacks. In May of 1778, Levi was warned by his neighbors of pending Indian raids in the area and advised to seek refuge in the nearby fort. Levi knew many of the Indians in the area, his wife being half Indian, and because of this Levi felt he had immunity from these Indian raids.

On the morning of May 12th, Levi started his mill as usual and then went to his cabin to get some breakfast. While at the cabin he took the time to mend his moccasins with a needle and thread before returning to the mill. He had been at the mill just a short time when he heard a strange sound outside. Forgetting about the warnings of his neighbors, he went outside to investigate the cause of these strange sounds, leaving his wife to operate the mill. He was just a short distance from the mill when a shot from an Indian rifle struck him in the heart and killed him. Mrs. Hicks hearing the shot and fearing for her life, ran to river, crossed it at the ford, and headed out running towards Fort Lytle. On her way, she encountered a settler on horseback. Hysterically she explained to the rider that Indians had attacked their cabin and shot her husband. After the rider had understood what she was trying to frantically explain, he quickly rode off to the fort to warn the settlement of an Indian attack. After he rode off, she glanced back over the trail where she had just come, and noticed for the first time that her son, about 10 years old, was following her. She then realized that during all the commotion she had forgotten about her children back at the cabin.

When she finally arrived at the fort, the men there refused to go in pursuit of the Indians until the next day. The following day the party reached Hicks' cabin and found Levi's body scalped on the spot were he was shot and killed. A young girl who ventured out of the cabin during the attack to see what the Indians were doing to her father, was hit on the head, scalped, and left for dead. The Indians left without entering the cabin, into which the little girl managed to crawl, and was found by the party sitting in the corner gibbering like an idiot. Her face and head were covered with clotted blood. In the cabin with her were two children lying on the floor crying, and an infant in a cradle, crying for nourishment. The scalped girl lived for a number of years, but not having adequate medical attention, she became feeble minded. No record of the oldest son that followed Mrs. Hicks on her death-defying escape was ever found.

In 1806 Levi Hicks and his family, together with Andrew Overturf and Samuel Smith, made their way up the Sinnemahoning River to settle in the Driftwood Area. John Jordon settled there several years previous to their arrival, becoming the first resident of what is now Driftwood. Andrew Overturf built a two story log Cabin near where the Bennett's Branch flows into the main river. Levi Hicks settled between First Fork and Second Fork (Bennett's Branch), on ground afterward known as the Shaffer farm, later occupied by Malden Wykoff. Here, Levi cleared about thirty acres of land. In 1812, Levi now 35 year old, sold this land to Jacob Burge who had settled next to him a year or two previously. After selling the farm, Levi moved on up the Bennett's Branch to the mouth of Hicks Run, and established a farm and engaged in logging. Levi floated the first log raft down the Bennett's Branch into the Sinnemahoning. Later he would become a pilot for Miles Dent and piloted a number of rafts from Dents Run down the Bennett's Valley into Williamsport.

Is the Levi Hicks who settled in Hicks Run about 1812, the son of the Levi Hicks who was killed at the mill in Spruce Creek? Would it be logical to assume that the apparent oldest son of Levi, who was killed by Indians, was named Levi after his father? Levi, the assumed father, was born about 1771. The boy, who escaped with Mrs. Hicks to Fort Lytle, was born about 1768, both dates having a variance of two or three years. There doesn't seem to be any existing records to indicate where Levi migrated from before coming to settle on the Bennett's Branch,

JOHN C. HICKS – OLDEST SON OF LEVI & REBECA HICKS. Picture courtesy of Virginia M. Hudsick.

nor does there appear to be any existing records to determine whatever happened to Levi's son who some judged to be 10 years old at the time Levi was killed. Was it just a coincidence that Levi came to settle at the mouth of Hicks Run, a stream named after Gershom Hicks? Many Hicks historians believe, but can not verify that Levi Hicks who settled on the Bennett's branch was the son of Levi Hicks, the brother of Gershom for whom Hicks Run was named.

Levi married Rebecca about 1799. They had eight children:

John C. Hicks - married Mary Elizabeth Conway

Jacob Hicks - married Barbara Hoover

William Hicks - married Elizabeth Woomer.

Jane Hicks - married John English

Margaret Hicks - married Ira Greene

Nancy Hicks - married George English

Hester Hicks - married John Smith, and

Polly Hicks - married Thomas Smith

THE END

WENNAWOODS PUBLISHING
RR2 Box 529c Goodman Road
Lewisburg, Pennsylvania
www.wennawoods.com
Journal of Samuel MaClay Published by John F. Meginness,
History of Brule's Discoveries and Explorations by Consul Willshire Butterfield
The Indian Traders of the upper Ohio Valley by John Arthur Adams
History of Northwester Pennsylvania
The Olden Time by Neville B. Craig
Journal of Samuel MaClay,
The Journal of a Two-Months Tour, Pennsylvania in the War of the Revolution
Michigan Pioneer and Historical Society - Vol 19
The History of Huntingdon and Blair Counties of Penna., by J. Simpson Africa published by Louis H. Everts of Philadelphia, Pa..
History of Mc Kean Elk Cameron and Potter Counties, Penn. - Beers.
Wilderness Chronicles of Northwestern Pennsylvania, the Olden Time Vol 1
Source - Michigan Pioneer and Historical Society, Vol. 19

The Morey Family

Seneca Land 1600's

The land in Pennsylvania west of the Alleganies in the 1600's was Indian Territory. Sometime about 1650, The Seneca drove the previous inhabitants, believed to be the Monsey Clan of the Lenni Lenape – relatives of Delaware Indians, from the headwaters of the Susquehanna. Seneca history refers to expansion of their territory as the "Great Conquest." However, many Seneca historians believe that their acquisition of these lands was accomplished as a result of negotiations, and at the time of white mans arrival here a number of Indians of various tribes, including the Huron, Tuscarora, and Lenni Lenape,

STATUE OF CHIEF
CORNPLANTER
OIL CITY, PENNSYLVANIA
Picture courtesy of
OIL CITY ARTS COUNCIL

inhabited these lands with and under the jurisdiction of the Seneca Nation.

When the first pioneers came to Second Fork to settle, they found the remnants of a number of Indian Lodges (villages) all along the banks of Second Fork (Bennett's Branch), together with a number of artifacts. The Seneca Nation was a member of a powerful Indian confederacy known as the Iroquois Confederation, quite often referred to as the Five Nations, later to be called the Six Nations when the Tuscaroras joined the federation.

Stanwix Treaty 1784: "The Last Purchase"

When the Revolution erupted between the American Colonies and England, the Seneca became allies with the British. This alliance proved to be a devastating disaster for the Seneca. General John Sullivan and his army, commissioned by General Washington, in the summer of 1779, led a scorched earth campaign against Seneca villages, farms, and animals. The once powerful Seneca were forced into submission. Washington's victory at Yorktown over English General Cornwallis, marked the end of the war, and beginning of the newly formed government of United States to take over and control the land. Representatives of the United States and the Iroquois meet in Rome, New York, and negotiated the 1784 Treaty of Fort Stanwix. This agreement could be more appropriately described as terms for surrender than a treaty. To the victor belong the spoils. The 1784 Treaty of Fort Stanwix, signed by Seneca Chief Cornplanter, was the final negotiation in which the Iroquois ceded all lands west of the Niagara River to the United States. The Pennsylvania portion of this negotiation was known as the "Last Purchase" and included lands in the following counties: Bradford, Tioga, Potter, McKean, Lycoming, Clinton, Cameron, Elk, Clearfield, Indiana, Jefferson, Forest, Warren, Armstrong, Clarion, Butler, Venango, Allegheny, Beaver, Lawrence, Mercer, Crawford, and Erie.

Entrance to Fort Stanwix National Park in Rome, New York.

Now unto the scene comes Robert Morris, Jr. Morris was the major financier of the Revolutionary War, a personal friend of George Washington, and a person who played an essential role in winning the war. He was one of only two people to have signed all three documents which created the foundation of the government of the United States: The Declaration of Independence, Articles of Confederation, and the United States Constitution. He also possessed extensive international trading and banking connections. Morris recognized the potential for a profit in these vast, resource rich lands in western New York and Pennsylvania. As a banker and speculator with powerful political connections, Morris relentlessly began to acquire these lands as a broker for a group of Dutch investors known as the Holland Land Co.

Massachusetts claimed the western part of New York as part of their land grant from England. This area would later be returned to the solvency of the State of New York. The Iroquois Federation also claimed title to the land. Morris purchased from Massachusetts this land in New York, which included approximately 3,750,000 acres, for the sum of $333,333.34. This purchase amounted to less than nine cents per acre!!! However, this sale was contingent upon Morris satisfying the Iroquois claim.

In order to quiet the Iroquois claim, on September 15, 1797, in Genesco, New York, Morris, represented by his son Tom, met with members of the Iroquois

ROBERT MORRIS

Federation which included Seneca Chief Cornplanter, Red Jacket, Governor Blacksnake, Farmer's Brother, and about forty other Iroquois chiefs and sachems. Several Commissioners represented the United States. This meeting would become known as the Treaty of Big Tree in which Morris purchased from the Iroquois their interest in this land which included land in Pennsylvania known as the "the Last Purchase" for the sum of $100,000.00, excepting 200,000 acres of land in southern New York that was set aside for an Indian reservation.

The Alien Act

NEW HOLLAND LAND CO. MUSEUM, BATAVIA, NEW YORK

Morris and the New Holland Land Co. were now confronted with one last obstacle before title of the land could pass to the Dutch investors. Only citizens of the United States could own land in the United States. To overcome this problem, the Dutch investors hired future Vice President Aaron Burr as a lobbyist. He was given five thousand dollars to sprinkle among New York legislators to assure passage of the Alien Landowners Act. This act became law in 1798, and allowed aliens to own land and enabled Morris and other American Holland Land agents to transfer this land to the New Holland Land Co. In 1801, the New Holland Land Company opened an office in Batavia, New York, and sectioned the total purchase into tracts and appointed land agents to sell this land for a handsome profit.

On December 16, 1811, the New Holland Land Company advertised in the form of handbills the sale of 140,000 acres of land which they designated as the Burlington Tract. This sale included land in both Mc Kean and Clearfield Counties. Later in 1843, Elk County would be carved from portions of both of these counties, Bennett's Branch being part of Clearfield County at the time of this sale.

Dr. Daniel Rogers was appointed by the New Holland Land Company as a land agent for lands located on the Bennett's Branch. In the spring of 1812, Rogers came to Summerson, located several miles below the village of Benezette, and built a rustic 16' x 20' cabin to serve as a land office. Years later, a large dam would be built here to splash log rafts and logs down the Bennett's Branch. Many local citizens refer to this site as Doctor's Rocks, an obvious reference to Dr. Daniel Rogers.

Leonard Morey 1812

In April of 1812, Leonard Morey, Captain Joseph Potter and William Ward, in response to New Holland's land sale, set out on a trip to Dr. Rogers' cabin on the Bennett's Branch to inspect these lands for possible settlement. They started out on horseback from their homes in Susquehanna County located in the northeastern part of Pennsylvania. On April 5, the third day of their trip, they reached Dr. Willard in the village of Newton in Tioga County, and by the fifth day they reached Butler's cabin on the North Fork of Pine Creek. Here they left their horses and ventured on foot to the headwaters of the Allegheny River and stayed that night with Mr. Heirs. The next leg of their trip took them down the Allegheny River where they spent one night with Major Lyman, and then continued to Canoe Place now known as Port Allegany. Here they departed the river and proceeded southward down the Portage Road, camping out on the way, to the head waters of Sinnemahoning to a place known as the "Howling Wilderness" to rest at the residence of John Earl. John Earl was the first resident of Emporium. He located in this area in 1810.

The following day the entrepreneurs proceeded downstream to John Spangler's place located two miles on the Emporium side of Sterling Run and then continued further downstream to Driftwood where John Jordon and Andrew Overturf had already taken up residence, becoming respectively the first and second citizens of Driftwood. The last leg of their journey took them up the Bennett's Branch to Dr. Rogers' small, primitive log cabin. The first land speculators have arrived. One has to wonder how they were received by the very few and very private original settlers. One-hundred thousand acres were up for sale, but only the most hearty and industrious folk would attempt to partake of the riches and freedom inherent in this new, uncivilized, foreign land.

The three men spent several days with Rogers while inspecting the lands, and apparently pleased with what they found, Leonard Morey and Caption Potter purchased property. Leonard entered into an agreement on April 15th to purchase a tract of land about a mile below the present village of Caledonia, while Potter purchased land near the mouth of Medix Run, known by many local residents as the Dollinger farm. The advertised terms of the sale was two dollars an acre which represented an enormous profit for the New Holland Land Company, with up to five years to pay, the first two years being interest free. Leonard, his oldest son Erasmus, and Captain Potter would return in September to make arrangements to bring their families here the following spring.

The Morey Family arrives 1813

On the 13th of February of the following year, the Morey family set out on a trip to relocate from Harford, in Susquehanna County, to Dr. Rogers' cabin. The Morey family included Leonard, his wife Phoebe, her invalid mother Betty Woodward Wheelock who was bed fast and unable to walk, and their six children: Balfour Erasmus – 17 yr., Eliza – 14 yr., Cephas – 11 yr., Selah – 7 yr., Emeline Ameneda – 3yr., and Eli born on July 4, 1812. Joining the Moreys on their trip here was Dwight Caldwell and his family along with Ichabod and Sylvester Powers, and William F. Luce.

The Morey family journeyed here via a different route than Leonard's first trip. This trip started by proceeding to the vicinity of Towanda and then following the waterways to Williamsport. Here they hired boatmen to ferry them up the river in canoes. We assume this route was chosen as it was an easier way to bring the families and what limited provisions and earthly belongings they were able to haul.

The river canoes the pioneers used were mostly constructed of wood although some of the more primitive ones were dugouts from large logs. These canoes were capable of a pay load of about eight hundred pounds. They were manned by two people, a bowman and a sterns man who would work in unison, using settling poles to push off the bottom of the river bed to propel the canoe forward.

The Moreys proceeded upstream from Williamsport, a trip they would make many times in the future for supplies in Jersey Shore. At Grass Flats on the Sinnemahoning, Captain Potter joined the entourage. On April 12th, two months after beginning their arduous journey, the travel weary pioneers reached Andrew Overturf's residence, a two-story, hewn log cabin located near the confluence of Second Fork (Bennett's Branch) and The Sinnemahoning.

The party pushed the canoes hard against the river's current, and about one and a half miles up the Bennett's Branch they encountered a small cabin belonging to Billy Nanny, located near the mouth of a small tributary entering the branch from the south side. Nanny had located here the previous fall. This small stream would become known as Nanny's Run. Another mile or so up the Branch they came to Thomas Dent's cabin located by Dent Run, not to be confused with Dents Run which is a bit further up the branch. The party's next stop was a small shack in what is now Grant. This was the residence of Ralph Johnson and his newly wedded wife, Rebecca Brooks, who had recently located to the area. The party moved on to what was then known as Sugar Creek Bottom, named for a large stand of sugar maple trees that once grew there near the mouth of Johnson Run. Here on a rainy April evening they made camp.

The next day, April 19, the Morey party arrived at Dr. Rogers' cabin. The Moreys, exhausted by the long arduous journey that had taken nearly two months, were exhilarated that they had finally arrived at Rogers' cabin. Also staying with Rogers were Amos Mix, the paternal grandfather of the famous movie star

Tom Mix, and his family. That evening the Moreys found their accommodations in the small cabin quite cramped.

Captain Potter, unlike Leonard, left his rather large family back in Susquehanna County, obviously intending to first prepare adequate living conditions before relocating his family here. Leonard and Potter had been long time acquaintances and it appears that the two decided to work together to help each other develop their homesteads. Leonard traded his land near Caledonia for bottom land near the mouth of Medix Run, next to Potter's purchase.

They built a crude canoe, packed it with some of their tools and belongings, and Leonard, Potter, Erasmus, and Cephas headed off to Medix leaving the other family members at Rogers' cabin. Upon arriving at Medix they constructed a makeshift shelter from a large hollow Buttonwood and began to cut and haul logs to the site of their new home. Once the cabin was started, Leonard returned to Dr. Rogers cabin on April 24th, to move his family and remaining provisions to the site of their new home. Pioneer cabins were generally small, being about 16' x 20' or less in size with a sleeping loft. The floors were split puncheon or logs hewed on one side and matched at the edges. The roofs were split clapboards held in place by weight poles. Logs were hand split rough timbers. Around the first of May the family moved into their new cabin and turned their attention to planting crops.

Although the weather was quite rainy and wet that first year, the Moreys managed to plant what precious seeds they had brought with them. They fully realized that their existence here depended upon a successful fall harvest. They planted corn and wheat and anxiously waited for it to ripen. Potatoes were planted in rotten stumps, as this didn't require the clearing of land to plant.

Early Pioneer Life

In the fall of 1813, the Moreys fortuitously had a successful harvest. Now the daunting task of grinding the raw grain into flour had to be accomplished. To meet this need, Captain Potter crafted a crude milling device by cutting a short hickory log and carving a bowl like depression on one end of the log large enough to hold about a peck of grain. A hardwood pestle was made to fit the depression in the log. The log was stood on end, with the depression facing up, near a small sapling which was trimmed and used for a spring pole. The pestle was attached to the top of the sapling. The person grinding the grain would then place the grain in the mortar, and seizing the pestle with both hands would thrust it with force into the mortar, crushing and grinding the grain. The spring pole would draw up the pestle again, and when released from the hands would be thrusted into the mortar. This process would be repeated over and over again until the grinding process of producing flour from grain was completed.

Fortunately the land here proved to be fertile. According to John Brooks, an early settler, the native grapes grew here as large as crab apples, yielding as much as fifty bushels from one vine. Also, Brooks claimed that native plum trees grew on the river bottom lands by the thousands and yielded large, luscious plums that were fit for the gods. In addition, wildlife in the surrounding forest was plentiful and included native Pennsylvania elk which once roamed in the woods of Bennett's Branch. The river and tributaries bubbled with trout and eels.

Erasmus and Cephas were known throughout the settlement as skilled hunters. This was a skill they more than likely learned early in life, as on many occasions the daily hunt decided what the family was having for supper. According to the early Clearfield County records, they killed a number of wolves for which the county paid $12.00 for each wolf. In March of 1853, Erasmus Morey and Peter Smith killed six full grown panthers in the Medix Run area. The largest one measured thirteen feet from the tip of the panther's nose to end of its tail. A panther's tail averages about three feet long. This same year Jack Long and his father Bill killed five panthers in this same area making a total of eleven panthers killed in 1852.

In September of 1813, the settlers along the bank of the Bennett's Branch became quite alarmed when they heard cannon fire off in the distance. Not knowing the cause or the source of the noise, they set out to investigate, thinking maybe it was an Indian attack on another settlement. Much later they would learn that what they heard was the cannonading of Perry's battle with the British on Lake Erie which resulted in American's first naval victory. Although the Indians here were generally friendly, there were many skirmishes between the settlers and Indians in Pennsylvania which continued up to the end of the War of 1812. In the 1790's in Sinnemahoning, Peter Grove and his small group killed eight or nine Indians who had tortured and killed his brother prior to the Treaty of Big Tree.

The Marriage of Eliza Morey 1814

In 1814, Eliza, the Moreys' oldest daughter at the age of 16, and Richard Geolott planned to get married. At this time there weren't any churches on the Bennett's Branch nor were there any residing squires or preachers. The couple, accompanied by Eliza's brothers Erasmus and Cephas, along with William Luce and Mrs. Caldwell, canoed 35 miles down the Sinnemahoning to Keating where they were married by Squire Lusk on June 19th. The return trip home via canoe was their two day honeymoon.

Richard and Eliza bought the land that Captain Potter was clearing for his homestead in Medix Run. Captain Potter had not been able to persuade his wife Lois to relocate to the wilds of Bennett's Branch. To this land the Geolotts made a number of improvements. Richard built a grand house for the times near where the future site of the railroad depot would be located. To this end he hired old Isaac Webb and George Bliss as carpenters, together with George Huller, Eben Stephens, Michael Oval, Joel Taylor and others, most of whom were pioneer settlers. They added amenities in the form of board and picket fences with fancy gates, and planted an elaborate flower garden that included many flowers not native to the area. In addition they imported and planted many trees which included Lombardy poplar, balm of Gilead, mulberry trees, and planted an orchard with a variety of fruit trees. The Geolotts literally created a showplace in the wilderness that many people, both friends and travelers, stopped to visit and admire.

Grist Mills

In 1815, Erasmus Morey traveled to the Kersey Settlement to help William Fisher build a community grist mill. This trip took Erasmus over a road that was cut in by William Kersey from the Meredith farm in Kersey to the mouth of Kersey Run, the current site of the town of Weedville. William Fisher had succeeded William Kersey as land agent for the heirs of Samuel M. Fox, the Fox lands comprising approximately 100,000 acres. Fisher built a grist mill with a sieve which replaced a crudely built mill that William Kersey had built for the convenience of the few settlers who had settled in the area together with offering an enticement to attract new settlers to the area. This mill was a community mill in that those bringing their grain to be ground were their own millers. The mill was destroyed by fire a short time later, leaving the settlers with the choice of resorting to primitive hand mills or traveling great distances to have their grain milled into flour until another mill was built.

Leonard Morey

Leonard Morey purchased on the 24th of November, 1815, from General James Potter, 379 ½ acres of land for $2,000.00 dollars ($5.25 an acre). These lands embraced the low lands in the vicinity of what is today the village of Benezette. This area was known as Potter's Bottoms, and previous to that time was known to the Indian's as Salt Lick which was obviously a source of salt at one time. Windy Bloom claimed that many of the old timers referred to the road leading to the Benezette Cemetery as Salt Lick

Hill. This being the same site that Sam MaCay, when surveying the Second Fork in 1787, noted in his journal the existance of an old log cabin believed to be the former residence of Major John Bennett for whom Bennett's Branch was named. Previous to being called Bennett's Branch, this tributary of the Sinnemahoning was called Second Fork. Erasmus Morey, in an interview when he was 92 years old, said, "When they first located here, corn hills that were cultivated by Bennett were still visible". The Major was quite a farmer for that time. It is said that he yoked his milk cows to plow and till the fields.

In April of the following year Leonard began making improvements to this property and built a house and small flutter wheel grist mill on a small stream that ran through Benezette and empties into Trout Run. In 1818, this mill was replaced with a larger, water driven mill capable of grinding seven to eight bushels of grain a day. Leonard spent much time at the mill grinding grain for customers, and when necessary provided them with room and board for their teams. Leonard continued to provide a milling service to the local settlers and ran a sort of bed and breakfast for travelers going up and down the Valley until 1827 when he sold his property and improvements to Reuben and Ebenezer Winslow.

ERASMUS MOREY
Picture courtesy
Looking For Ephraim
Helen Dixon Hughes

Erasmus Morey

In the winter of 1820, January 4 to be exact, Erasmus Morey at the energetic age of 24, embarked on a journey by foot to visit his grandfather Ephraim Morey in Charlton, Massachusetts, his birthplace.

Leonard originally lived in Charlton and had moved to Harford, located in northeastern Pennsylvania prior to relocating to Medix Run. Erasmus began his trip by following the same path back that they made on their first trip here to Canoe Place, now called Port Allegheny. Here, instead of following the Allegheny up stream as they had originally come, he traveled northward to Batavia, New York, and generally eastward to his final destination - Charlton. We assume he chose this route to make several visits, as he noted in his journal a Mr. G. Geolott, who may have been Richard's uncle, and there were probably additional visits as many of the early settlers of the Bennett's Branch were from the area on Erasmus's route.

Ephraim, a veteran of the Revolutionary War, was 74 years of age at the time of Erasmus's visit. Ephraim enlisted for the war in May, 1775, while a resident of Pomfret, Massachusetts, and served seven months under Captain Ebenezer Mosely at Roxbury, Massachusetts, until December 9, 1775. He enlisted again while residing at Oxford, New Hampshire, under Captain Jeremiah Pos, and assisted the wounded Captain off the battlefield. Ephraim, according to the Revolutionary Rolls, had obtained the rank of Captain. Ephraim survived four wives. Anna Goodell, his first wife, was Erasmus's grandmother.

Erasmus's return trip home took him from Charlton to Holland, the place of his residence before coming to live on the Bennett's Branch. He then followed the same route home as the family did in 1813. Erasmus walked an astonishing 1100 miles during brutal winter months on this trip to visit his grandfather.

Leonard, Cephas, and Erasmus

Also in 1820, Leonard Morey traveled throughout the northern portion of Pike County canvassing the resident settlers with a petition to form a new township. In 1821 the court granted Morey's wish to carve a new township from Pike Township to be named Sinnemahoning. The settlers were so upset with the name of their new township that they petitioned the court to have the township renamed to Fox Township in honor of Samuel M. Fox. In 1832, part of Jay Township would be formed from part of Fox Township.

In 1821, the Moreys opened the first school of record in Elk County. The school, presided over by Cephas Morey, was held in a two-room community building in Medix Run.

When the pioneer settlers of the Bennett's Branch first arrived here, and for a number of years afterwards, the closest source for supplies was Jersey Shore. The main means of transportation was by river canoe. Erasmus would say later in life that on many occasions ice would form on the canoe poles making it impossible to row, and when this happened, the canoe had to be beached and the supplies backpacked home through the woods. A story told by an ancestor of the Denisons, said that Starr Dennison, an early pioneer settler in Spring Run, would yoke a team of oxen to a sled when the Bennett's Branch froze over and travel down the Branch to Jersey Shore for supplies. In about 1820, a trading post opened on the West Branch, which created a need for a road.

Leonard Morey and Peter Aaron Karthaus entered into an agreement on July 13, 1822, to cut a section of road from Karthaus to Medox Run. The road was to be eight feet wide and made passable for sleds, with bridged and dug ways to make the road suitable for travel. Some of the old road contracts would specify that the road had to be wide enough for two wagons to pass. Morey was paid $12 a mile, and he cut his section of the road from Medix to what was once known as the 13 mile tree, head of Mosquito Creek. The road was opened in 1822. Prior to this road, there was a road cut in 1817 or 1818 from Shawville to Medoc Run, referred to by the settlers as a bridle path as it wasn't passable with a team and wagon. This road is believed to have been cut out by people from Clearfield and more than likely followed an old Indian trail.

The First Post Office

ELK COUNTY'S FIRST POST
OFFICE – MEDIX RUN,
PENNSYLVLANIA – POST MARK
– BENNETT'S BRANCH
Picture Courtesy
Helen Dixon Hughes

Medix, or Medoc Run as it was then called was the site of Elk County's first post office - Post marked Bennett's Branch. Beer's History of McKean, Elk, Cameron and Potter Counties states, "The first mail carried through Elk County was carried by William C. Walch from Milesburg to Smethport in 1828." The first post office was at Richard Geolott's house, where the Barr Railroad depot was once located. The post office was called Bennett's Branch. The second post office in Elk County was presided over by Vine S. Brockway at his house in Caledonia, and the third at Kersey where James Green was sworn to fulfill the duties of postmaster L. Morey, March 12, 1828. Erasmus Morey was the second postmaster at Bennett's Branch, commissioned July 4, 1828. This office was changed to Caledonia when Zebulon Warner took charge. In another section Beer refers to Erasmus's appointment as postmaster, as succeeding the pioneer postmaster at that point. Erasmus was later postmaster in Ridgway in 1837 and at Clearfield in 1854.

Although the first mail route through Elk County was established by William C. Walch, it would be safe to assume that the first post office to send and receive mail was the Bennett's Branch Post Office, and this post office could have functioned as early as 1822, the date the road from Karthus to Medoc Run was completed - being the same road Leonard had worked on. The first stop on the initial mail route entering the county was at the

Bennett's Branch Post Office, which would indicate that the mail was delivered over this road. In 1828, the Milesburg Road was completed. This main artery entered the county at Caledonia, and became the route of the mail, causing the Bennett's Branch Post to be relocated to Caledonia.

All this presents two questions: first, the actual date the mail service was started in Elk County, and second, who was the pioneer postmaster that Erasmus replaced? Gladys A. Tozier's book "Tozier and Allied Families," tells us that Leonard Morey, while riding a mail route on horseback, would knit and finish a pair of socks on each ride. We conclude that Leonard Morey was the first post master in Elk County and that the mail route could have begun as early as 1822

About four years later, on September 4, 1824, Erasmus married Mary E., the daughter of Fredrick and Nancy Hoyt Weed. Weedville is named after Mary's family.

Erasmus Morey

The following is from the pen of Erasmus describing his wedding day:

At this time marriage people had to get married the best way they could. More than still remembering his trip down the river to attend his sister Eliza marriage,
Now, I will tell you how I got married after living to the age of 24 years myself and concluded it as not good for me.

The venerable Preacher was to have a meeting at the house of one of the neighbors. The parties put on their Sunday best and started afoot about 2 miles to the meeting.

Nothing of note occurred till preaching was over then I Erasmus Morey, with sparkling eyes and glowing cheeks proudly paraded in position, while by his side, with warm soft hand sweetly trembling in his, stood the angelic form of the youthful Miss Weed.

We were soon pronounced man and wife .When the time came for going home we started up return trip home up to where Weedville now is, we went alone -- had no particular invited guest.

We had that day but few roads and far between - no carriages, few wagons and I have as yet to learn that it did not answer all and every purpose.

(Signed)
Erasmus Morey

July 4, 1826

July 4, 1826, marked the 50th anniversary of the birth of our nation. The Gelotts and Moreys planned a big event to celebrate, a very special event in that most of the settlers were either second or third generation of those who had participated in the Revolutionary War. Liberty poles and a flag pole were raised, together with a pavilion of sorts erected in the orchard, covered under the bower of green branches, with tables spread out beneath to accommodate the festivities. The events included the reading of the Declaration of Independence, with various orations to take place in a new barn which was clean and large enough to host the event.

However, a dark cloud hovered over the celebration. Phoebe, Leonard's wife, was quite ill and felt that the noise and confusion of the day would be too much for her. She reluctantly asked Richard if he would take her to Henry Mead's to spend the day. There was a close relationship between the Morey and Mead families. Two of Phoebe's sons married Mead girls, Cephas married Fanny Amanda Mead, and Selah married Lucy Mead.

Richard and Phoebe rode to the Mead homestead on horseback. Phoebe rode behind Richard, and on the way she said, "Richard I feel as though I am going up there to die", and went on to tell him what she wished to be done in case such a thing would happen.

The next morning Phoebe passed away at the age of 61, the mother of eight children, who in the early years of homesteading on the Bennett's Branch had endured many hardships and struggles in the family's herculean effort to make a new life in the raw, untamed wilderness.

In 1830, the Gelotts sold their farm to Eliza's brother Erasmus and moved to Holland, New York. Several years later they would return to Bennett's Branch to settle about a half mile down creek from Medix. After living here a few years they sold this farm to Samuel Overturf and moved to Chautauqua County, New York. They had eleven children which included two sets of twins. Eliza died August 18, 1850, at the age of 52. Richard moved to Iowa in his later years to live with his son.

First Election of Elk County Officers

The first election for Elk County officers was held on October of 1843. Chauncey Brockway, John Brooks, and Reuben Winslow were the first elected County Commissioners of Elk County. In this same election, Leonard Morey, a Whig, was elected as one of three county Auditors. Later, in May of 1844, Leonard was appointed Commissioner's Clerk. The first order of business was to establish the location of the county seat. As clerk, upon the decree of the Commissioners, Leonard gave notice the Honorable Judges of the Court of Common Pleas and the several courts, in and for the County of Elk, and notified the other officers of said county, that the Commissioners continue to designate the school house near the house of Hezekiah Warner in Jay Township, whereat to open and hold the several courts for Elk County. On September 16, 1844, the first grand jury of Elk County was convened in Caledonia. Selah Morey, whose occupation was listed as a farmer, was a member of this jury.

A power struggle developed on where the court house was to be located. The commissioners held meetings at the Erasmus

Morey home in Ridgway to resolve this issue. After several months of debates and considerations, Ridgway was selected based upon proposals for donated land for the county seat.

Jay Township's first election as part of Elk County was held on February 27, 1844, and Leonard Morey was elected Supervisor and his son Selah Morey was elected Justice. As one of the first resident tax payers of Jay Township, Leonard Morey was listed as an owner of a silver watch, which at this time represented a status symbol amongst the local citizenry.

Leonard Morey died on May 19, 1845, at the age of 72 and is buried next to his wife on a hill side in Medix Run in an unattended family cemetery plot. Leonard made his own tombstone by carving his initials "L M" on a native stone.

As a young man, Leonard Morey began and maintained a diary over his lifetime. He had the fortuitous insight to accumulate and save many documents pertaining to the happenings of the early times on the Bennett's Branch, together with the formation and development of Elk County and local townships. These papers, stored in a trunk, were passed to Erasmus

In his later years Erasmus who lived to be 95 would often reminisce about life as a pioneer settler. He wrote a number of articles, together with furnishing information for numerous articles pertaining to the olden times, often referring to his father's journals. Many of these articles appeared in the Democrat under the title of the Early Times. Beers in the History of McKean, Elk, Cameron and Potter Counties, states, "Mr. Morey (Erasmus) and John Brooks are two pioneers who have done the part of good citizens in preserving records of pioneer times, which otherwise might be lost forever". Erasmus's earliest recollection was attending the funeral service with his parents, of George Washington in 1799. On this historic occasion, Erasmus would have been about three or four years of age.

Leonard Morey was undoubtedly lured here by the availability of the inexpensive land and the abundant resources the area offered. He moved his family from a civilized part of the country to live in an uninhabited wilderness, and endured many hardships and heart breaking struggles as a pioneer to carve out a home on the banks of Bennett's Branch. He played an important role in the development of the area and in so doing he became one of the most prominent citizens among the early pioneers on the Bennett's Branch.

Erasmus passed on May 24, 1891 (born 1796), thus coming to end the last true pioneer settler of the county. The following is his obituary as it appeared in the Du Bois Courier Express on May 29, 1891:

Erasmus Morey, aged 95 years, died on Sunday, May 24, at the residence of his daughter, Mrs. D. H. Kerr at Benezette. The funeral ceremonies were held at Mt. Zion Church, in Jay Township on Tuesday afternoon. Mr. Morey was probably the oldest man in Elk County and had resided in the vicinity of Benezette for the last 78 years. Mr. Morey buried his wife over 20 years ago and is survived by but three of the seven children who formerly composed his family.

THE END

Ps - Medix Run was once known as Medoc Run, was named after the Medoc family, who settled here in 1800 for two years, and later moved to Franklin, Pa. One member of the family was active in the Oil City Historical Society. The family made frequent trips back to Medix. The family originally came here from Bellefonte, Pa.

History of McKean, Elk and Cameron Counties - J. H. Beers
"Looking For Ephraim" by Helen Hughes
Tozier and Allied Families by Gladys A. Tozier
Journal of Samuel MaClay Published by John F. Meginness,
Wilderness Chronicles of Northwestern Pennsylvania, the Olden Time Vol 1
History of Pennsylvania by Egle
Elk County Democrat – Elk County Historical Society
The Genealogy of William A Winslow and Gladys M. Burke by Robert Nay
The Treaty of Fort Stanwix 1784 – Henry S. Manley
History of Clearfield County by Lewis Cass Aldrich, 1887
Raymond Nelson
WENNAWOODS PUBLISHING www.wennawoods.com
RR2 Box 529c Goodman Road
Lewisburg, Pennsylvania

THE LEWIS FAMILY

A story of Love, Thievery, and Longevity

The Lewis Lewis family history is steeped in both richness and diversity to rival the most epic Hollywood production. From an Oxford graduate in England to a shoot-out on the banks of the Sinnemahoning, the story of the Lewis family presents a most dramatic story of pioneer life in Pennsylvania.

Lewis & Jane

The story begins with Lewis Lewis' birth in Wales in 1736, the son of Thomas Lewis. At the age of twenty-one, Lewis Lewis graduated as an engineer from Oxford University in 1757. Sometime after graduation, he and his two brothers, David and William, together with relatives by the name of Williams, immigrated to America. Lewis' early travels in this new country took him to Dillsburg, and here he made the acquaintance of Jane Lewis, the youngest of four children of Thomas and Mary Dill.

Dillsburg was founded upon land owned by Jane's grandfather, Caption Matthew Dill, who received this land as a grant from the Provincial Government of Pennsylvania for exemplary services to the Colony. Jane never knew her father, Thomas, as he died the same year she was born. Mary, Jane's mother, remarried Caleb Beal, who fathered and raised Jane, together with her two brothers John and Thomas, and her sister Mary.

When Jane first met Lewis, she was a robust Irish lass of seventeen, sort of an inquisitive tomboyish type with boundless energy. It would obviously appear that Lewis's life as a surveyor, traveling the countryside of Pennsylvania's untamed frontier, cast an irresistible lure of adventure and excitement that a girl with Jane's spirited personality couldn't resist. Although Jane was fourteen years younger than Lewis, in 1767, Jane and Lewis were married and moved to Carlisle to settle.

Here in Carlisle, Lewis began his life as a noted pioneer surveyor on the Colony's western frontier, surveying up and down the banks of the Juniata River. This area at that time exposed both the inhabitants and travelers to many perilous risks from both Indians and wild animals such as panthers and wolves that roamed the area. All the land west of the Alleganies was Seneca Indian Territory. The French and Indian War had just ended a few short years before, and the Revolutionary War was about to erupt. Indian hostilities in Pennsylvania would not be extinguished until the end of the War of 1812.

The Pioneer Surveyor

On September 13, 1773, Lewis received an appointment as District Surveyor in the Nittany Valley Area by the Provincial Government of Pennsylvania. Lewis would be the first person to practice his profession as a surveyor in and around the area of Centre County. Centre County was then part of Cumberland County. His surveying work included laying out the town of Lewistown, a town that some claim was named after him.

About this same time, Jane gave birth to the first of their ten children, Jacob Henry, born in York County. Sadly, two of their children died in infancy. Sara, the second oldest was born in Bellefonte, which at the time was in Northumberland County. Thomas, the third child was born on August 27, 1776, the same day that George Washington's troops were being soundly defeated in the Battle of Long Island at the beginning of the Revolutionary War.

Lewis's position as District Surveyor kept him quite busy traveling and surveying up and down the Susquehanna and Juniata Rivers. Quite often, when Thomas became of age, Lewis took him as a helper in surveying lines in the headwaters of the

Susquehanna. While Lewis was attending to his work, Jane was kept quite busy having children and raising a family.

In 1785, Cumberland County encompassed a rather large portion of Pennsylvania. It is interesting to note that the county's records for this year show that Lewis and Jane were assessed for a horse, two cows, and two Negroes. Unfortunately, the records do not indicate where in the county the Lewis family lived at this time.

Tragedy Strikes

Lewis was seriously hurt in an accident, being hit by a falling tree and suffering severe internal injuries. In 1791, Lewis died in Lewistown as a result of these injuries. Just prior to his accident, and shortly after the birth of their youngest son Davy, Lewis and his family moved to a 300 acre parcel of land in Bald Eagle Nest, once the residence of the famous Indian Chief Bald Eagle. This is the present site of Milesburg.

At the time of his death, Lewis and Jane's names appeared on the tax rolls on numerous parcels of land located throughout Central and Western Pennsylvania. It was a common practice to pay a surveyor in a portion of land for services rendered. The Lewisses owned land in Northumberland, Bedford, and Cumberland Counties. These counties where much larger then than they are today and included land in present day Clearfield and Elk Counties.

Jane, now forty-two years old, was a widow faced with the enormous undertaking of raising a family that included eight children ranging in ages from Jacob the oldest, at 18 to David an infant. In addition, Lewis died without a will.

Jane's neighbor, Frederick Leathers, had purchased his property in 1790, and here he cleared the land and established a farm. Leathers, a widower, lost his wife about the same time Jane lost Lewis. In 1792, Jane and Frederick decided to poll their resources and were married. In addition to farming and lumbering, Frederick built and operated a distillery.

Frederick died in 1796, leaving Jane a widow for the second time within four years. Jane inherited the farm and some money, together with the responsibility of providing for the family, which included running the farm. Sometime earlier, Jane had taken on an Indian woman and a young girl by the name of Cynthia, believed to be the daughter of the Indian woman, to help with family chores. Davy, who loved his mother dearly, although quite young, worked at odd jobs to help support the family.

Jane, unable to make ends meet on the farm, followed in the foot steps of her older sister Mary, who like Jane had lost her husband early in life, at the age of thirty-six, and had taken up general nursing and midwifery to help support the family.

Sometime between 1800 and 1802, Jane moved from her farm in Bald Eagle to Chinklacamoose, in Lycoming County. On March 25, 1804, this same area would be carved from Lycoming County to form Clearfield County, which remained annexed to Centre County until 1808. The Clearfield County had one large township known as Chinklacamoose, and Jane and her sons (Thomas and David) appear on the list of the first taxable inhabitants of the Township. Lewis Lewis' name appears among a list of the single freemen of the county, and although he died in 1791, his name probably is listed because his will was still in probate court.

Jane's son Thomas married Cynthia Ellis on February 12, 1804, and moved to a stone house in Roopsburg, located near Bellefonte. This same year Thomas signed on to guide to a surveying party hired to mark the boundary lines of Clearfield County. A man named Webb, believed to be Isaac Webb, was a surveyor in this party. He would later settle on a thousand acre tract of land, founding the village of Force.

Thomas Lewis's great, great, great grandson, Samuel Lewis McCracken, would state quite confidently that he had Indian blood flowing in his veins, and was quite certain that Cynthia was the daughter of the Indian woman. This probably is the origin of stories about there being Indian graves on Lewis Mountain.

In the 1950s to 1980s, Jack Van Alstine, who spent many years searching for the lost gold shipment, found a rock near the base of Buck Point, near the stream of Trout Run, upon which was chiseled the

Could this rock have been a marker for the old Clearfield County line?*

date of "1804." Could it be that the surveying crew who made the original survey of the Clearfield County boundary line marked this date on the rock? This date rock is in the general proximity to the old Clearfield County Line.

In 1806, Thomas, Andrew Overturf and Levi Hicks ventured up the Susquehanna to the present site of Driftwood, where they planted corn for shares during the spring and summer months. Tom would return back to his home in Roopsburg to spent the winter months with his family. This went on for several years. Andrew Overturf would settle in Driftwood a few years later, becoming the second citizen of Driftwood, and Thomas would acquire a parcel of land of about 290 acres on Rock Hill, located on the top of a mountain overlooking the village of Medix Run.

When Jane moved to Clearfield in 1802, she brought her late husband's distillery, and here in Clearfield she established the first brewery and distillery in the area on a site which is presently the intersection of Brewery Hill and Third Street. In addition to operating the brewery and making moonshine, Jane continued to practice the profession of midwifery.

Jane took her work as a midwife quite seriously, and as a result of her dedicated and faithful service to the citizens of the area, she became very popular and well liked. Affectionately known as

"Granny Leathers", she had a hand in the births of nearly all the first born citizens of Clearfield County.

While the Lewis family was living in Clearfield, Davy, Jane's youngest son, now seventeen, ran off to Bellefonte and joined the army. He deserted soon after enlisting, and several months later in Carlisle, he reenlisted in Captain William Irvine's Company of U.S. Light Artillery under the assumed name of Armstrong Lewis. Shorty after he joined this unit, Davy's true identity was discovered and he was court marshaled. Double enlistment was a crime, and desertion was a hanging offense. The military court convicted him of desertion and sentenced him to be executed before a firing squad. Some accounts claim that his mother, Jane, attended the court marshal pleading for clemency for her son. Perhaps it was because Davy was a minor, but in any event, Davy's sentence was reduced to prison time. Shortly following his conviction, he escaped from prison. David Lewis was now a wanted man.

Davy Lewis the Robber

Running out of places to hide in Centre County area, Davy fled to Burlington, Vermont, and became involved with a gang of counterfeiters. In the early 1800's, paper currency was in the form of bank notes drafted on various banks throughout the country and much easier to counterfeit than today's currency. Davy and his gang were not just content to pass off phony bank notes, but in addition, they engaged in a spree of robberies and hold-ups in Vermont, Canada, and New York.

In Troy, New York, sometime about 1810, David met and fell in love with Melinda Blankenburg. However, Davy's love life didn't interfere with his thieving activities. Soon after he met Melinda he attempted to buy a horse from an army general, using a counterfeit bank note for payment. This obviously angered the general, who made an asserted effort to have Davy captured and locked up in the Troy jail house.

Born with a silver tongue, Davy, could charm the pants off a preacher's wife. One Sunday morning, as Davy sat locked up in the Troy jail, the only guard was the jailer's daughter. Davy began working his charm on the girl until he finally persuaded her to unlock the cell door and let him escape. He kissed the jailer's daughter good-bye. As the faithful citizens of Troy sat in church singing hymns as a tribute to God, Davy boldly strolled down Main Street to find his true love Melinda. Together they rode off to Albany to get married, leaving only a brokenhearted jailer's daughter and a cloud of dust for a posse to follow.

In Albany, David and Melinda, were married, and while there Davy used his charismatic charm to finagle a private invitation to a party given at the home of the wife of the noted entrepreneur John Jacob Astor. Davy charmingly relieved the wealthy partygoers of their jewels and other valuables, letting them know they were robbed by Davy Lewis the Robber. There is a scene in the movie of *"Butch Cassidy and the Sun Dance Kid"* that mimics this real-life escapade of Davy Lewis.

Davy comes home

On September 28, 1811, Davy and Melinda became the proud parents of a daughter they named Mary Jane, who assumed the nickname of Jemima. The following year a second daughter, Kesiah was born, but unfortunately, shortly after giving birth, Melinda

One of several caves the Lewis Gang allegedly used as a hide out in Carlisle, Pa.
Courtesy of the Cumberland County Historical Society.

died. Sometime about 1812, Davy decided to return home to Carlisle, the site of his birthplace, with his two children and marry a woman by the name of Margaret.

The estates of both of Jane's deceased husbands, Lewis and Frederick, were still in probate. In 1812, Jane, as an executor of both of these estates, moved back to Centre County where she could administer first hand the final disposition of these properties and where she could again renew her relationship with Davy and see her two new grandchildren.

In Centre County, Jane took up residency in a house located on the turnpike between Pleasant Gap and Axeman, near an old known landmark called the "Old Red Barn." Jane's son Caleb lived nearby in Milesburg and worked as a laborer at the Harmony Forge.

In Carlisle, Davy's activities as a robber intensified. The Lewis gang found a secluded cave in the vicinity of Carlisle that they used for a hideout and went on a reign of terror robbing travelers and stagecoaches in the local area. Posse after posse pursued this elusive outlaw without success, as Davy would make it back to the hideout undetected. To this day, many treasure hunters search Davy's old hideout, believing that there are thousands of dollars worth of gold and silver coins buried near the cave.

On one occasion in neighboring Adam County, a posse was formed to go after "Davy Lewis the Outlaw". Davy, hearing of the plan, thought he would have a bit of fun and joined the posse. When the search ended in failure, Davy expressed his disappointment and rode off on his way. A few days later, the sheriff received a letter which read, "I trust you did not find Lewis, the Robber, to be such a bad companion after all", signed Davy Lewis. (In 1813 Carlisle was in Cumberland County)

Another time, in Penn's Valley, Davey decided to rob a boarding house. As he entered the boarding house he was greeted by an elderly lady, who asked what she could do for him. Davy asked if she could make change for a five dollar note. The idea was to watch where she hid her money and then rob her. To his surprise, she broke down in tears, explaining that not only didn't she have any money, but the constable was coming this very day to serve her with an eviction notice for back taxes. Davy, feeling sorry for her situation, gave her the twenty dollars she needed to pay for the back taxes with instructions to get a written receipt. As the constable rode back down the trail after being paid, Davy sprang from his hiding place in the bushes with guns drawn and relieved the constable of the twenty dollars and then some.

Quite often when Davy was roaming the country sides of Centre County, he would take time to visit his mother. The Sheriff of Bellefonte, because of these frequent visits, hearing that Davy might be in the area, would often raid Jane's house trying to capture the elusive outlaw. On a number of occasions, Davy would be awoken from a sound sleep by a friendly neighbor warning him of a pending raid. Grabbing his coat and hat, Davy would tear out on the fly, galloping down along Spring Creek, leaving only a warm bed and a cloud of dust for the Sheriff and his deputies to follow, and would escape up over Sugar-loaf Mountain. Later in his life, Davy would reflect back on these foiled attempts to capture him and laugh, referring to them as fox hunts, adding that the fox always got away.

Davy Lewis, described as a handsome, good-looking chap, standing about 5'10" high with a muscular physique, was a very polite, well-mannered person and an exceptional conversationalist with a likeable sense of humor. Certainly he was not a person you would take for a villainous outlaw and hold-up man. As Davy's reputation grew as a notorious robber, he was often referred to by many citizens throughout the countryside as the Robin Hood of Pennsylvania. While newspaper accounts referred to him as "Davy Lewis the Robber," Davy himself preferred to be called the "Equalizer." He was a shrewd outlaw, as he often shared his loot with those who supported his unlawful activities. This personality coupled with his unique, flamboyant flare for practical jokes and pranks was amusing at times causing many of his antics to become legendary.

The guest of Davy Lewis

One night a lonesome traveler by the name of Simmons was traveling between Bellefonte and Lock Haven. Having been forewarned that Davy Lewis was in the area, he cautiously traveled the back trails, and as nightfall was approaching, he noticed a light coming from a small cabin. Thinking that this would be a good place to spend the night, he knocked on the cabin door and was greeted by a smiling, muscular man who invited him in. That evening the host fixed Simmons something to eat and offered him a drink. Later, while they were playing cards, the traveler confided to his host that he was carrying a large sum of money and was worried about robbers being in the area. The next morning the host bid Simmons a safe trip and said, "By the way, tell all your family and friends that last night you were the guest of Davy Lewis."

Another story exists about Davy. Philip Benner was returning from Pittsburgh one day with a considerable amount of money that he had received as payment for the sale of iron ore when Davy stopped him on the road. Being quick witted, Benner gave Davy a friendly greeting by saying, "Oh, Mr. Lewis! You are just the person I was hoping to meet. Things have been mighty tough lately, we are having problems finding good ore, the ore market is down, and we desperately need some money or we are in big trouble." Davy looked Benner in eye, thought for a brief moment, and gave him a sum of money. Davy's decision may have been influenced by the fact that his brother Caleb worked as a laborer at the Milesburg Forge for Joseph Miles and Joseph Green.

Davy was once again captured in the early part of 1816 and sentenced to six years in the Philadelphia Penitentiary. In September of 1819, Governor Findlay pardoned Davy, commuting his sentence from six to 3 ½ years. Shortly after being released from prison, Davy teamed up with a man by the name of Connelly who was a mean, vicious character. They went on a crime spree in Dauphin, Perry, Cumberland, York, Adams,

Franklin and Bedford Counties holding up stagecoaches and robbing Conestoga wagons and travelers traveling the roads and turnpikes of central Pennsylvania. These assaults instilled many fears and anxieties in those persons planning to travel in this area.

When Governor Findlay ran for reelection in 1820, a man by the name of James Duncan had hand bills printed and passed out to the citizenry of the Commonwealth, announcing that Governor Findlay had pardoned this terrible outlaw – Davy Lewis. The poster listed all the crimes that sent Davy to prison together with a copy of his signed confession. Heister defeated Findlay in this election and many people felt it was the result of Duncan's handbills. Governor Heister was obviously appreciative, as he appointed James Duncan as Auditor-General of Pennsylvania on April 2, 1821.

David and his gang were captured on October 1819, when they tried to rob a Pittsburgh merchant on a mountain turnpike and were locked up in the Bedford County Jail. They broke out of the jail, but within a short time were recaptured and returned to the Bedford Jail. Davy managed to escape for a second time, and this time in order to cover his escape, he freed all the prisoners in the jail. In the midst of all the confusion, Davy made a clean get away.

Davy's freedom, however, was short lived, as several months later he was caught in an attempt to rob the house of Mr. Beshore. As reported by the Republican Compiler, Lewis and Connelly were seen in the area of Mr. Beshore's residence several times arousing suspicion about their intentions. The neighbors devised a plan that if a robbery attempt was made, the victim would blow a horn. The trap worked and Davy was caught, but Connelly managed a clean get away. However, Davy, being the escape artist he was, broke out of jail a short time later, again free to continue on his crime spree.

Tom & Jane homestead Rock Hill

While Davy was having his run-ins with the law, Thomas, in 1817, moved to a 290 acre parcel of land that he had previously purchased on Rock Hill, which was located on the top of a mountain overlooking the village of Medix Run. Thomas family at this time included his wife Cynthia and their three children: Ellis, Lewis, and George Washington Lewis. Also coming here to settle with Thomas was his mother Jane and Cynthia's mother, the Indian woman. This settlement would soon be known as Lewis Mountain as Thomas gradually converted the forested land into fertile farm fields.

Jane was undoubtedly relieved to escape the commotion Davy was causing in and around Centre County. A few years after settling here, Jane, at the jaunty age of seventy years, married for the third time to Ree Stevens.

Take me if you dare

Davy decided to pay a visit to a popular and well-known general store on the corner of Front & Market Streets in Harrisburg, where people would gather on a regular basis to visit and discuss current affairs, local news, and general gossip. Davy would often visit local saloons, boarding houses, and meeting places such as this to catch up on the local news and seek information on local shipments and stagecoach schedules. Davy would sit and quietly listen and learn what was happing.

On this particular visit, the conversation turned to the risks and dangers of traveling the local roads due to all the robbers and cutthroats operating in the area. Several of the braggarts began telling the crowded store how they would bring this Lewis character to his knees if he ever tried to rob them. Davy, amused by their bold statements just could not restrain himself any longer. He sprang to his feet, with both guns drawn, and shouted, "I'm David Lewis the Robber, Take me if your dare." The store erupted as if hit by a sudden bolt of lighting, putting the entire crowd to flight, with people bumping into each other, falling and stumbling over tar barrels and butter churns, desperately trying to put as much distance as possible between them and this vicious robber. Davy, with a smug laugh, holstered his pistols and calmly walked out the front door, leaving the store in a state of shock and confusion.

In about the 1820's the Centre County area was rapidly developing economically as a result of the discovery of iron ore marking the beginning of the iron industry in United States. As a result of this booming economy many people were migrating to Centre County area seeking work, creating the need for goods and supplies. Hammond & Page became dominate merchants of the day to supply the needs of these people. They imported their supplies and merchandise on horse drawn Conestoga Wagons over the mountains from Philadelphia.

Hammond & Page was expecting a shipment of three wagon loads of goods from Philadelphia, and as the wagon train crossed Seven Mountains just a few miles from Potter's Mills, one of the wagons broke down. Being late, the teamsters decided to leave the wagon, and drive on to John Carr's Tavern at Potter's Mill. Lewis and Connlley had been following the wagon train, and they seized the opportunity to help themselves to the goods in the abandoned wagon. Apparently not satisfied with their haul, they proceeded on to Potter's Mills, like a fox chasing a rabbit to rob the remaining two wagons. Carr saw the outlaws approaching and was ready for a fight. Lewis, seeing he was out gunned, took off like a fox being chased by a pack of hounds. The table had turned, and now they were being chased by the same people they intended to rob. They out ran their pursuers except for one person by the name of Paul Lebo who managed to catch up to them. Connelly captured Lebo, and had him nearly choked to death before Lewis intervened. Unlike Connelly, Lewis was not a violent man, and would use force only in self defense.

Posses on their trail

A messenger was immediately dispatched to Bellefonte with news of Lewis's raid at Potter's Mills. The citizens of Bellefonte quickly organized and devised a plan to capture the Lewis gang. They formed two posses, one under ex-sheriff William Alexander, and the other under Centre County Coroner James McGee. Alexander would proceed down Nittany Valley, collecting a posse as he went, and go by the way of Great Island, following the river up to Bennett's Valley. The McGhee posse, including John Mitchell, William Armor, Paul Lebo, Peter Deisal (a one arm man) and Joseph Butler (sheriff of the county the following year), was to travel overland through the Quehanah area towards the current site of Benezette. The goal of both posses was to converge on Davy's mother, Jane Lewis, cabin on the Bennett's Branch.

The McGhee posse made it to Karthaus the first night. Here McGhee obtained the services of Andy Walker, well-known hunter of the local area, as a guide. Also joining the posse here were William Hammond, John Koons, Samuel Karnell, and Peter Bodey. Before proceeding the next morning, they received news that the Alexander's posse captured McGuire, a member of the Lewis Gang, and had both Lewis and Connelly on the run.

The next night, on the 29th of April, 1820, the McGhee Posse got lost and had to camp overnight. On the following day the posse found their way to the confluence of Trout Run and Bennett's Branch. Walker and Karnell went to Jane Lewis' Cabin looking for Davy. Satisfied that neither Davy nor Connelly was there, they rejoined the posse. That night the posse proceeded down the Bennett's Branch to Shepard's place on the Driftwood Branch. Shepard told the Posse that two men fitting the description of Lewis and Connelly had had breakfast there that morning. The Posse, accompanied by Shepard, followed the trail of the two men eight miles up the Driftwood Branch. When they caught up to the two suspects, they were disappointed to find that they were not Lewis & Connelly.

Shoot and be dammed! We will shoot back

The posse then proceeded back down the Driftwood Branch, and between the present site of Driftwood and Sinnemahoning they encountered John Brooks gigging for eels. Brooks told the posse that he had seen Lewis and another man in the morning. Brooks joined the posse and together they had proceeded a short ways downstream when they heard gun-fire. Brooks guided them to a spot on the mountainside overlooking the river where they observed Lewis and Connelly shooting mark. McGhee shouted out a demand for them to surrender. Lewis' answer was quick and to the point. "Shoot and be dammed! We will shoot back." Who fired the first shot is not certain, but one of the first shots fired hit Lewis in the arm, shattering the bone, causing him to fall severely wounded. Connelly tried to escape across the river, but just as he was approaching the far bank, a bullet fired by Peter Deisal struck the rim of Connelly's abdomen causing his entrails to protrude.

Lewis and Connelly were taken by canoe down the Sinnemahoning to Great Island to the mouth of Bald Eagle Creek, arriving there on the 2nd of July. Here Connelly died as a result of his wounds and was buried in the Great Island Cemetery. David Lewis was taken on to Bellefonte where he was incarcerated in the local jail. His arm was a mess from the gunshot wound, and many of his friends advised him to have it amputated. Dr C. Curtin, a skillful surgeon, offered his services but Davy refused. On several occasions when Davy would look out the window of his jail cell, probably while planning an escape, he was known to have said that he could see on the far mountain top where he buried the haul from his last robbery. Judging from David's past, this may have been a prank, but if it was, it was his last prank, David Lewis the Robber died several days later of gangrene in the Bellefonte jail on July 13, 1820. David is buried in Milesburg.

The boundless energy and enthusiasm Jane exhibited in her youth remained with her throughout her life. At eighty years plus, Jane made a trip on horseback from her home in Benezette Township to Louisville, Kentucky, to visit her oldest son Jacob. Jacob, who hadn't seen his mother for years, was walking down Main Street of Louisville, when Jane come galloping into town unannounced with her long gray flying in the breeze. Jacob turned to his companion, and in a state of amazement said, "That old lady is my mother."

Jane Dill Lewis Leathers Stevens, a mother of ten, survivor of three husbands, a person who lived through the Revolutionary War and the birth of this nation and a person who was one of the first pioneer settlers of the Benezette area - departed this world,

JANE'S GRAVESTONE

at the ripe old age of 92 in 1842. The energized life of Granny Lewis had come to an end.

Ellis Lewis, Thomas's son, inherited the Lewis farm. Ellis was born in Bellefonte, and came to Rock Hill with his father to live. Although Ellis had no formal education due to the lack of schools in the area at the time, he learned farming, lumbering and other useful skills while working with his father. Ellis became a millwright at the age of 20, a profession he practiced for a number of years. In 1851, Ellis was elected treasurer of Elk County and held a number of other local offices as well. The Lewis farm passed on to his son, Winfield Scott Lewis, one of Ellis and Anna Butler Michaels eleven children. Winfield Scott Lewis, described as a person whose usual attire was buckskins adorned with a coonskin hat, married Ella Younger. Their only child, Ruie married Raymond Irwin. The Irwins were the last of the Lewis line to reside on the Lewis farm.

The Lonesome Grave?

The old Lewis homestead has vanished into the past. The site has been heavily timbered and stripped for coal. All that remains of the Lewis Farm is a crudely carved gravestone indicating Jane's gravesite. Over the years, this site became known as the Lonesome Grave. However, this name is a bit misleading, as there are a number of unmarked gravesites next to Jane's grave. Although some of the people interred in this family cemetery can be identified, Thomas is not one of them.

Where is Tom?

While returning home from Jersey Shore to consult a doctor concerning an intestinal disorder, Thomas suddenly took ill and died. The crew and passengers in the canoe were horror stricken. Thinking he had died of the plague, they quickly put to shore and buried Thomas on a bank of the Susquehanna River near Jersey Shore. Thomas's son, upon learning of his father's death, traveled to the burial site and placed a marker on Thomas's grave. Thomas Lewis died on April 10, 1855, at the age of 68.

Sometime in or around the 1970's, James Ross placed a marker near Jane's gravesite. Inscribed thereupon is "GRANNY

HISTORICAL PLAQUE
Installed by Jim Ross

LEATHERS, JANE (DILL) LEWIS, LEATHERS - STEVENS, 1750 - 1841 AGE 92. The census records indicate Jane was born in 1750. However, some family decedents claim that Granny Lewis lived to be 106.

THE END

1. History of McKean, Elk and Cameron Counties - J. H. Beers
2. The Legend of Lewis the Robber - Newville Historical Society.
3, History of Centre County
4. Shoot and be Damned - by J. Marvin Lee
5. History of Clearfield County by Lewis Cass Aldrich, 1887
6. Outlaw David Lewis Terrorized Area - Grit #47 - October 1, 1978
7. Pennsylvania's Robin Hood - Lewis the Robber by Ann E. Diviney
8. Descendants of Thomas Lewis - Family genealogy - author unknown
9. Lewis Genealogy by S.L. McCraken
* Picture 1804 – was enhanced to been show the date.

ANDREAS OBERDOFF – ANDREW OVERTURF FAMILY

The Dutchman

Andreas Oberdorf(f), a German immigrant, came to the confluence of Sinnemahoning Creek and Second Fork to settle about 1804, and became one of the very first settlers on the Bennett's Branch. He was quite well known throughout the area by the early settlers as the Dutchman, as the elderly German spoke with a strong accent. His family and friends affectionately referred to him as Uncle Billy.

Andrew (Andreas) resided in the village of Weilheim, Germany, before coming to America. Weilheim is located at the forks of the Main and Tauber Rivers in the Township of Lendebach, Weilheim County, in the ancient Providence of Palatinate, a hilly, forested land that borders France.

The Americanized version of the name Andreas Oberdorff is Andrew Overturf. The origin of the name Oberdorff is one who dwells in the upper village. (ober-up / dorf – village). The name Oberdorf is a common German name with many variations in spelling. One can often determine by a particular spelling in what part of Germany that person once lived.

Persecution + Taxation = Emigration

The Providence of Palatinate, from the late 1600's and into the eighteenth century, was a hotbed of numerous military entanglements and conflicts that imposed many trying times upon the distressed residents of the province. King Louis XIV, of France, during the war of the Grand Alliance, plundered and destroyed farmlands in the eastern portion of the Palatnate. During the French Revolutionary and Napoleonic Wars; the Palatnate lands on the west bank of the Rhine were incorporated into France.

During a period of time in the seventeenth century, the Eastern Palatnates were Catholic, ruled by a Catholic Prince, while the western Palatnate was ruled by five or more Protestant Counts known as Co-Regents, each with its own religion, mostly dominated by Lutherans and Reformed Calvinists. Weilheim County was Lutheran. The rulers of each of these political regents imposed their religion upon their subjects. This religious turmoil and persecution caused many additional problems for the residents of the province.

The people of the Palatnates were severely depressed economically by many burdensome taxes. There were land rents, grazing fees, hunting fees, watch fees, plowing fees, food tax, tax on second hay harvest, tax on hand work rendered, the Prince's personal tax, chimney tax and water tax. Taxes were only limited to the imagination of those who ruled the land, and if one didn't have a creative imagination, he would copy a tax in an adjoining province. There was the Manumission Act which in essence was a tax for those migrating from the province. Peasants worked from the dark hours of early morning to the dark hours of the evening to obtain a meager existence at best.

This impoverished land, so miserably burdened with taxes and plagued with religious persecution, caused many Germans to emigrate from the Fatherland. Many of these immigrants became early German settlers of Pennsylvania. They were known as Pennsylvania Dutch. There were so many German immigrants coming to America that many citizens of Pennsylvania, including Benjamin Franklin, were seriously concerned about the impact they would have on the English Commonwealth.

During this period of mass migration from Germany, there were agents known as Newlanders. These Newlanders would roam the countryside signing up people for passage to America then known as New England. These Newlanders normally worked on a commission and to induce people to sign up they would quite often exaggerate the opportunities and life in the Promised Land. Many peasants entered into arrangements, indenturing themselves and members of their families for passage to the New World.

Migration Decision

Andrew Overturf decided to migrate to America and bring his family with him. On January 17, 1772, he indentured himself and his six children to Hannah O'Scullion in Philadelphia, for a term of two years, two months. They were to serve as apprentices to learn the trade of making leather breeches.

On March 30, 1773, Andrew, now a widower with six children applied to the Count of Lowenstien, to whom he was subject, for a Certificate of Manumission to give him and his family permission to leave the County of Wertheim. There doesn't appear to be any records to document the names of Andrew's six children who came to America with him. It is generally assumed by most historians that two of the six children were Johann Michel and Henry. Another may have been Michel, as future records in America make a reference to Micheal. However, some think that Johnann Michel and Michael may have been the same person. One family account claims that one of the children was a blind daughter, but there doesn't appear to be any evidence to substantiate her existence.

In April 26, of 1773, Andrew received from his father-in-law 210 florins. A florin is a unit of German currency in the form of gold and silver coins. Of the 210 florins, he had to pay a 5% Manumission tax amounting to 10 ½ florins, plus an additional 20% supplement tax on the balance of 199 ½ florins. The ironical situation in Andrew's case was that if he had just ½ florin more, he would only be required to pay 10%, as all amounts 200 florins, or more, were subject to a 10% tax; less than 200 florins, the tax rate was 20%.

Journey on the Rhine

Andrew departed Weilheim and left behind a debt of 819 florins. The family began their journey to America from Weilheim and traveled down the Rhine River which flows north to Rotterdam, Holland. This leg of their trip took about four to six weeks to complete. One account contends that the Overturfs encountered a number of tollhouses on the river. One could only imagine that traveling from one political district to another or from one country to another at this time in history could cause a number of frustrating delays. After arriving in Rotterdam, the family was again detained, waiting for the ship *Hope* to sail for America to the port of Philadelphia.

The Atlantic Passage

Sailing from Europe, across the Atlantic to America in the 1700's was a long hazardous trip, exposing the passengers to many hardships and dangers. The sailing ships of the day were generally small and in most cases severely over crowded without adequate food and provisions. In addition, the Atlantic Ocean could become very violent in the fall, as experienced in the Mayflower crossing. A typical crossing averaged about eight to twelve weeks. Thew Johnson and his family, early settlers on the Bennett's Branch claimed they were on the water for 63 days when they sailed from England to Philadelphia. Consequently, disease was common and conditions were harsh. A number of passengers died. In one case in the 1820's one ship lost over 25% of its passengers. If that weren't enough, in many cases crewmembers would steal the passengers' luggage.

On October 1, 1773, the hazardous and long ocean journey began. The Overturfs sailed from Rotterdam on the Ship *Hope*. Listed on the ship's manifest were Andreas (Andrew), Johann

Michael Oberdorff, and Johann Berhart Rau. The ship manifest included males over sixteen, without reference to women and children under sixteen. Johann Michael was born 1757, which would make him over 16 at the time of the ship's departure. The other Overturf children were under sixteen. Johann Berhart Rau applied for a Certificate of Manumission at the same time as Andrew, and more than likely the Rau family accompanied Andrew and his family from Weilheim.

Naturalization 1773

When the Overturfs finally arrived in Philadelphia they had to go through a process of naturalization, swearing their allegiance to England and becoming subjects of the King. The next step was serving out their indentureship making leather breeches under the stewardship of Hannah O'Scullion.

Andrew Overturf (Andrew Oberdoff) acquired 100 acres of land in Northampton County that was surveyed in 1774. In 1850, there was another Andreas Oberdorf who immigrated from Weilheim to Philadelphia. It would appear, based upon the limited amount of creditable information available, that this land was acquired by the Andrew who is the subject of this story. There doesn't appear to be any known evidence linking these two Andrew Overturfs, although a relationship probably does exist.

Freedom Fighters

War and the fight for freedom were no strangers to the Oberdorfs. Now, the battles held hope for the future. Andrew Oberdorf served seven months in the Revolutionary War under Captain Wagone in the 2nd Batten, 7th Company beginning June 21, 1780. He was discharged from the Pennsylvania Line on September 27, 1780, for physical disability.

Andrew's son Michael served in the war as a private in the 8th Battalion in Lancaster County in 1781 under Christian Shenk Sr.

Andrew's son Henry Overturf served in the Revolutionary War from the age of 16 to 21.

Family Man (Settling Down)

On April 4, 1783, Andrew married for the second time to Elizabeth Barbara Fuchs in the Trinity Lutheran Church in Lancaster, Pennsylvania. This union brought forth five children. The first child, a son Johannes (John), was born to Andrew and Elizabeth on May 27, 1784. John was baptized August 27, 1784.

In 1791, Andrew was operating a gristmill in Selinsgrove, Pa. The tax records indicate he was assessed for 200 acres of land, two horses and a cow. Andrew sold the mill to Major Anthony Selin. The mill, later known as Schnures Mill, operated until about 1920. His son Michael also appears on these same tax records.

Shortly after 1791, Andrew and his immediate family disappeared from the tax records for a period of time, as they apparently returned up the Susquehanna into the wilderness of Pennsylvania. One account by a descendant claims that Andrew lived on the Island of Cue, opposite Muncy, Pa., some time between 1791 and 1804. Beer, in his history of Elk and Cameron Counties, states that Sinnemahoning was surveyed on lands originally owned by Overturf and Shaffer about 1805, which passed into the hands of Philps & Dodge in 1816 and later became the property of Lyman Truman. We could assume that Andrew may have resided at Sinnemahoning before moving upstream.

Sometime between 1804 and 1806, Andrew and Thomas Lewis came to the Driftwood area to plant crops for shares during the summer months. The two would return home during the winter months; Thomas Lewis to Bellefonte, and Andrew probably to either the Island of Cue, or Sinnemahoning.

Driftwood 1806

In 1806, Andrew, along with Levi Hicks and Samuel Smith, came up the Sinnemahoning Creek to settle. Andrew built a two room log hewn cabin on the left side of the river near the confluence of Bennett's Branch and the Sinnemahoning, becoming the second resident of the village of Driftwood. The first known resident of Driftwood was John Jordan who settled across the river from where Uncle Billy built. Jordan was a noted hunter, who claimed to have killed ninety-six elk, and who could catch enough fish in twenty minutes to feed his family for an entire week.

River Canoes

Most of the early pioneer settlers to the Bennett's Branch came by river or Indian canoes; however, a few did come by foot or on horseback following the Indian paths and trails that ran along the banks of Susquehanna River and her tributaries. River or Indian canoes were propelled up stream using two wooden setting poles with pointed steel ends, one by the bowman in the front of the canoe and the other by the steersman in the rear of the canoe. By pushing their body weight against the riverbed in unison, they would push the canoe forward against the current. On a good day, two proficient canoe men could travel fifteen to twenty miles upstream, with a total payload of up to a ton.

Keeper of the Gate

When Andrew Overturf built his log hewn home in the wilderness, at the entrance to Bennett's Valley, then known as the Second Fork, he established himself, so to speak, as keeper of the gate for the early arriving settlers to Bennett's Valley. The Dutchman's cabin was a regular stop for those proceeding up the Bennett's Branch, as well as those traveling on up the

Sinnemahoning. It was also a favorite stop for those who enjoyed the homespun stories of the area's famous Dutch raconteur

A few miles upstream on the Bennett's Branch at the mouth of Dent Run, Thomas Dent settled a year or two after Andrew. Thomas married Andrew's daughter Elizabeth. John Earl stopped to visit the Dutchman in 1810, when he came up the Sinnemahoning to settle in what was then known as the "Howling Wildness" and become the first settler of the area now known as Emporium. Leonard Morey, Dwight Caldwell, and their families, together with Idchabod and Sylvester Powers, William Luce, and Captain Potter stayed overnight at Uncle Billy's on their way up the Bennett's Branch to settle.

Andrew first came to the Driftwood area about the same time Clearfield County was annexed from Lycoming County on March 26, 1804. Prior to this county redistricting, the entire Bennett's Valley was within the boundary of Lycoming County. In 1813, there was a legislative act establishing Lawrence and Pike Townships from Clearfield County's original township – Chinklamoose. This act created a new election district in Clearfield County, and Andrew's cabin was designated as the election house. Andrew's house was most likely selected because most of the settlers in the Valley knew the old Dutchman and where he lived. Later, in the 1830's, the biggest part of the land comprising Lawrence and Pike Townships would become Elk and Cameron Counties.

The Preacher and the Dogs

The Methodist Church of Sinnemahoning may be said to date back to 1810, when James Allen, a preacher, surveyor and general utility man, was sent by Coxe, McMurtrie & Co. to survey Rich Valley. F. J. Chadwick wrote a history of Methodism for this part of the country for the Emporium Historical Society. Mr. Chadwick referred in his writing to an incident that occurred at Andrew's cabin in Driftwood around 1820.

He (James Allen) came to the country and saw the destitution of the people with respect to spiritual privileges, and his soul was stirred within him to do something in their behalf. He proposed to hold a preaching service at the house of Mr. Overturf. Andy consented and sent out far and near, notifying his neighbors; for by this time quite a good number of people had settled around him. The Sunday for the appointed service arrived. The worshipers gathered in, bringing their dogs and guns, for it was scarcely safe to travel without them. Besides, as game was plentiful, it was expedient for them to be always ready to supply their tables by improving the opportunities that an occasion might offer. The congregation was seated – the service commenced – the text announced – and the preacher fairly engaged in its elucidation, when the dogs that were outside startled a deer, and drove him rapidly by the house. In an instant the whole pack was in pursuit. The congregation, forgetful of the proprieties of the occasion; forgetful of the courtesy due the minister; forgetful of their solemn obligations and their eternal interest, sprang to their feet, crowded out of the house, and joined in rapid pursuit. Overturf alone remained within the house, for he was temporarily disabled with rheumatism or some other indisposition. The preacher was, of course, filled with perfect astonishment and disgust, and lifting up his hand, and heaving a heavy sigh, he exclaimed: "It is all in vain!" meaning the attempt in which he had engaged to spiritualize these people. Andy, supposing he referred to the pursuit of the deer, responded: "Oh, perchance they may cat'h him yet".

A.W. Gray, sometime later, wrote and published this same incident, which had greatly amused the local residents, in the Democrat newspaper. Here is his version:

Perhaps brief sketches of history may interest some of the many readers of the Democrat, I will relate an incident which serves to illustrate the rude and uncultivated manner and habits of the primitive settlers of the Sinnemahoning Country, among the first settlers at the junction of the Driftwood and Bennett's Branch near where the present thriving town of Driftwood is situated, lived a Pennsylvania Dutchman, whom we will designate as "uncle Bill". The progeny of "Uncle Billy" are largely interspersed with the present inhabitants of Bennett's Branch, all the way from Driftwood to Benezette, and are among the best elements to society of the children of Uncle Billy. One daughter only remains and she is truly in sear and yellow leaf of life, having served out the allotted three score years and ten more than a decade since. That daughter is my authority for the following narrative. At the time I write, she was a blooming maid just gushing into womanhood. Uncle Billy lived in a rude log house on the bank of the stream, consisting of two apartments, designated respectfully as the kitchen and the room. At long intervals a Presbyterian Minister by the name of Barber, was wont to wend his way from the Big Island, as it was then called, up the West Branch and Sinnemahoning to the settlement at Driftwood, then called Second Fork to hold religious meetings. As Uncle Billy's cabin was central, and more capacious than the others, services were held in his rooms. On this occasion the reverend gentlemen in black made his appearance in the settlement on one fine Saturday evening. The announcement was promptly made for preaching next day, (Sunday). Accordingly as the hour drew near, the church goers donned their toggery, which at best was but scanty habiliments, and congregated at Uncle Billy's to hear preaching. The service was duly opened in approved orthodox style, and the minister was just warming up in his subject, when the melody of hounds was herd on hilltop. The excitement of the chase was too fascinating for the congregation, and forgetful of the occasion, men and women, all rushed from the house and joined in the hunt, except Uncle Billy, who was too rheumatic and lame to join in the chase, but he hobbled to the door and seated himself with his back to the speaker. The minister quite chagrined and mortified in a despondent tone remarked, "It's all in vain, in vain". Uncle Billy intent on the hunt and misapprehending his meaning, replied in his broken English: "I does not know by sure I tinks dey vill victim dem bees goot dogs, dere I Jordan's drive, and Coleman's bitch after im, and den tere is dem Jordan poys, dey been hell hounds der sclres". As Uncle Billy predicted, the deer was captured. History is silent, but by the light of tradition, we learn the minister never visited Sinnemahoning again for the purpose of preaching to the natives.

As a foot note the author added: Uncle Billy, the Hero of the above narrative, was the   veritable Andrew Overturf, who was introduced to our readers in the first of our Historic sketches.

The daughter referred to in the narrative, now deceased was Mrs. Betsy Dent, relic of the late Thomas Dent, who has many descendants now living in Elk, Cameron and Clinton Counties.

The author of the original article in the Democrat, A.W. Gray, was well known in Elk County, whose former wife was a daughter of Mrs. Dent, and consequently a grand-daughter of Uncle Bill – Andrew Overturf.

The Children

Andrew's son Henry from his first marriage and one of the 6 children who accompanied him to America, was born in 1761, in the village of Wertheim. Henry married Maria Chute, who was born about 1775. While residing in Union County, Pa, Maria gave birth to a son named Samuel on November 5, 1812. Shortly after Samuel's birth they moved to Clearfield County, and resided in what is now Benezette Township.

Samuel Overturf may have been a converted Quaker. He married Olivia Woodworth. Olivia, born in Clearfield County,

Pennsylvania on March 23, 1821, was a Quaker of French Nationality. Olivia's brother William P. Woodworth was born in what is now Cameron County in the year of 1821. (His wife Jane Miller was also born in Pennsylvania) in the year of 1828. Samuel and William were friends. In the spring of 1857, Samuel moved to Butler County, Iowa.

In addition to Andrew's six children who came from Germany to America with him, Andrew and his second wife, Elizabeth Barbara Fuch had five children: Andrew, John, Elizabeth (Betsy), Susannah, and Catherine.

Andrew's son Andrew married Hannah Jordon, daughter of James and Mercy Embry Jordon. Hannah's occupation was listed as a weaver, according to a list of the taxable inhabitants, dated Nov. 20, 1821, prepared by the Clearfield County Commissioners. They had six children: Martha (Massie) married Marmaduke Johnson; Elizabeth first married Thomas Hallen then married George Smith; Polly married Reuben Miller; Andrew married Elizabeth; James married Delihah Barr; Hannah married Benjamin Johnson.

Andrew's son John (Johannes) married Mary Jordon, Hannah's sister.

Andrew's daughter Elizabeth married Thomas B. Dent. They had four children: Thomas Jr., Andrew, William, and Miles Dent who became a noted lumberman and founder of Dents Run.

Andrew' daughter Susannah married William Shepard.

Andrew's daughter Catherine married James Mix, the ancestors of the famous cowboy movie star Thomas Mix. They had five children: Hezekiah, Ann Elizabeth, Solomon, Henry, and James J.

A Dutchman's Legacy

Andreas Oberdorff, having lived a hearty four score plus years, died January 1, 1821, leaving a number of descendants to carry on the Overturf name. Andrew, the Dutchman, was a family man, born in Weilheim, Germany in the 1730's during a time of unbearable governmental depression and religious persecution. He was a man so desperate for freedom and opportunity that he indentured himself and his six children for over two years to obtain passage to America. The name Andreas Oberdorff, a German immigrant, changed to Andrew Overturf, a Pennsylvania Dutchman. He served in the Revolutionary War for a cause which he sincerely believed: freedom and independence. He was an early settler on the confluence of Sinnemahoning Creek and the Second Fork, in the wilderness of the Pennsylvania Western frontier. His home was the site of the first organized religious service in the Driftwood area, and served as the first election house for the first organized Township elections in Bennett's Valley.

THE END

History of McKean, Elk, Cameron, and Potter Counties by Beers
Elk County Democrat (no date available)
Pennsylvania German Pioneers for the County of Wertheim by Strassberger & Hinke
Pennsylvania German Immigrants 1709-1786 – Edited by Don Yoder
History of Clearfield County, Pennsylvania – Edited by Lewis Class Aldrich
Probate, Elk Co. Will Books 1845 – 1916; Elk County Register of Wills 1851-1890;Docket V.A. 1844-1868
Early Records of the First Reformed Church of Philadelphia – Edward F. Wright
Special thanks to Lauren Brantner – for information furnished
Eva Caylor Gemology of the Johnson family

THE DENTS

Thomas Water Dent III came from England to settle on the Bennett's Branch about 1811. He married Elizabeth "Betsy," the daughter of Andrew and Elizabeth Fush Overturf, who had preceded Dent here by several years. Andrew Overturf was one of the very first settlers on the Bennett's Branch, settling at the confluence of Secord Fork and the Sinnemahoning, becoming the second resident of what would become known as the town of Driftwood. It would appear that Thomas may have been influenced to settle here as a result of this marriage.

MILES DENT
6-03-1834 - 3-18-1899
Picture courtesy of the Story of the Sinnamahoing

The newlywed's pioneer cabin was just a few short miles upstream on the Bennett's Branch, a short distance below the mouth of Mix Run. Thomas would later move up the Branch near the mouth of Nanny's Run where he would build and operate a saw mill. Thomas and Betsy were blessed with four children: Thomas Jr., Andrew, William, and Miles.

Nanny's Run was named after William Nanny who settled at the mouth of the run just prior to Thomas. Beers, in his book, described Nanny as the first instance on record where a single person represented both sexes of the goat. One might assume that on a given day you could call Nanny either William or Billy, depending upon you point of view.

A prominent businessman, Thomas Dent, played an active roll in area politics. He served as the Justice of Peace for a number of years, a position much more prestigious than today. In 1846, he was elected Elk County Auditor receiving 203 votes. Three years later he replaced Wilcox as County Commissioner and in this capacity issued a $100.00 six month note to James Halliday and Davidson, to build the Elk County Jail. On January 30, 1848, the construction of the jail was completed, with a cost override of $6.25 for extras.

MILES DENT

Miles Dent, the youngest son, was born at the Dent homestead on June 3, 1823. As a boy, Miles received what education he could from what limited resources the pioneer schools had to offer. In 1850, Miles married Lydia Miller, a daughter of Daniel and Mary Miller, for whom Miller Run was named. Miles acquired a large parcel of land stretching all the way from the mouth of present day Dents Run to the headwaters of the stream. This acquisition included several thousand acres of land containing one of the finest stands of virgin pines on the Bennett's Branch. Here at the mouth of this stream, which would bear his name – Dents Run, Miles began a rafting and logging operation that would create the village of Dents Run. His home, known as the "Dents' Mansion," was built on a hillside overlooking the valley and was the largest house of its day on the Bennett's Branch.

In a written account in the form of a letter, believed to have been written by Zula Conners, whose family was among the first residents of Dents Run, she recalled this anecdote about the Dent family. When Miles Dent first located to Dents Run, one day he was called on business over night and told his wife if the cow did not come home before dark not to milk it because there was a panther reported in the woods nearby. At this time, the Dents had two children: Isaiah, three years old, and Warren just an infant. When the cow came home, Mrs. Dent took Isaiah, leaving Warren in his crib, and went to the barn to milk the cow. When she returned to the cabin, she was shocked to find a big Indian lying in front of the fireplace with a tomahawk by his side. She was scared but had heard that if you were good to Indians they would not hurt you. They could not communicate as neither could understand the other's language. She provided him some lunch, and about a half hour later he left. About five years later, the Indian passed through Dents Run with a group of other Indians and paid the Dents a visit. Since his previous visit he had learned to speak English. He told Mrs. Dent that five years ago he had been in a rain storm and stopped at the cabin to get dry.

THE MAJESTIC PINES

The choice pine trees in Dents Run valley were located on the flat mountain tops where they grew exceptionally tall and straight, and could be timbered without breaking when they fell. This was very important as many of the logs cut from these majestic pine trees by Dent were trimmed into spar logs, built into rafts and floated on down the Bennett's Branch to Baltimore to be used by ship builders as mast poles on sailing ships. Some of these spar logs were floated all the way up to New England to be used by shipbuilders.

Some spars cut by Dent were used as mast poles on sailing ships. Above pictures shows a typical most pole measuring 112" in circumference at the main deck. Picture courtesy of Maine State museum

To access this premium stand of pine trees, Dent built roads on both sides of Dents Run Valley from the heart of the village to the mountain tops to be able to skid the logs down the steep mountainsides to two raft landings: one located just a short distance above, and the other just a short distance below the mouth of Dents Run stream. Here many of these huge logs were trimmed into spars, and assembled into rafts to be floated down the Bennett's Branch. Traces of the roads Dent built are still visible today, but all that remains of the majestic pine trees that once dominated the landscape of Bennett's Valley's mountainsides have long since vanished, leaving only a few weathered and rotten stumps as a reminder of the majestic pines that once grew in Bennett's Valley.

Emmett Lord was the chief spar maker on all of Dent's works, and Jake, Bill, and George Miller were his principal helpers. Jake English, Andrew Overturf, and Allen Barr were regular pilots. Ed Powers and his wife kept the camp and Mrs. Powers' sister helped with the cooking. Murt Hayes was the village blacksmith who ran a custom shop for a number of years.

THE LARGEST SPAR LOG

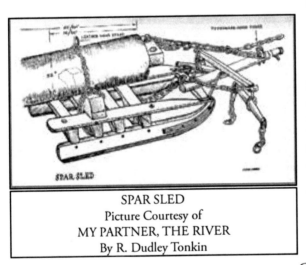

SPAR SLED
Picture Courtesy of
MY PARTNER, THE RIVER
By R. Dudley Tonkin

The largest spar cut by Dent was over one hundred feet long and contained five thousand board feet of lumber. It required three teams of horses teamstered by George Billings, Sam Woodring, and Ed Mix (The father of Tom Mix) to haul the huge spar to the edge of the steep mountain top. One team was sufficient to take the spar down the mountain, but the teamsters thought this was a very dangerous undertaking. While they were standing around discussing the best way to get the long spar down the mountain side, along came Dent who saw the situation and said if they were afraid to take log down the hill, he would take it himself. As Dent was descending the steep mountain, the big log got a bit lively, picked up speed, and pushed the team as it went.

Dent was able to keep the log under control until he neared the foot of the hill, when suddenly the log jumped the bank. Miles leaped to safety, but the big long spar plummeted down the steep hill, dragging the sled and team of horses with it. It was quite a calamity: one horse broke a leg, but fortunately both Dent and the big log escaped injury. It took quite an effort by the entire crew to recover the log. The injured horse was hauled back to the village on a sled and slung up in the barn to have its leg set. The leg bone knitted together, but the horse remained crippled, never to work in the woods again. The spar was loaded on top of a raft and floated down the river to the market at Marietta.

On one occasion, Jake English was piloting a raft of spars down the Sinnemehoning to Marietta with Levi Hicks as his steersman. When the splashes from the big dam did not provide enough flood to float the raft, the raft and crew laid up at Fulton's Eddy for about ten days until heavy rains raised the river high enough to proceed. Due to the long delay, part of the crew, including Ike Smith, Hank Mix, and Miles Dent decided to return home.

On their way to the train station to return back to Dents Run, they made a stop at a saloon located just across the tracks from the train depot. This was a stop they had made many time before on previous trips as it was a convenient place to wait for the train. One of the Dent's crew mentioned to the inn keeper, "You realize that of all the times we have stopped here, you have never offered up a free round," The inn keeper, in a sarcastic tone replied, "Now, what respectable saloon owner would offer free drinks in his own establishment to a bunch of wood hicks?" Miles Dent overhead this comment. Miles was known as a man of extraordinary strength, stood about six feet two inches tall, weighed approximately 200 pounds, and had huge strong hands. As Miles quietly listened, he decided to have a bit of fun. Lying outside near the entrance of the saloon by the railroad tracks was a frog (railroad switch) that weighed about 600 pounds. Miles went out, picked up the frog, brought it in and laid it lengthways on the bar, and turned to his crew and said, "Come on boys, let's go over to the depot and wait for the train." The inn keeper was frantic. "What I am I going to do? What I am I going to do?", he cried. Then realizing the joke that had been played on him, he announced, "Free drinks on the house for wood hicks." He begged Miles to return the frog to where he found it. They had several drinks, and when they finished, Dent exited the saloon carrying the frog.

RAFT OF SQUARE TIMBERS
(Story of Sinnamahone – Huntley)

In 1850, rafting pine spars down the Sinnemahoning was a flourishing business. About this time the first saw mill in Williamsport sprang up, and grew like a big wild fire, driven by the huge demand for sawed boards. Williamsport would become the "Lumber Capital of the World," a position that it retained for the next thirty to forty years. Consequently, the demand for pine saw logs was enormous.

When logging began on the Bennett's Branch, logs were cut and taken to landings on the banks of the branch to wait for spring rains to provide enough water to float them downstream. In addition to the rain, splash dams were built

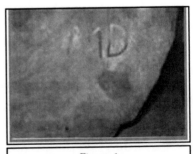

Figure 1
This picture shows the end of a log, found on the branch, stamped or branded with the initials "MD". This is believed to be the brand or log stamp of Miles Dent. Picture courtesy of Ralph Harrison

near the mouth of almost every tributary of the branch. During a log drive, water would be released from these dams, or as the hicks would say "breaking the dam", to create a flood to help float the logs on down to Williamsport. Each logging operation had it own personalized stamp or brand. Log saw logs were branded on both ends so they could be identified at the mills. Figure 1 shows a brand believed to use by Miles Dent. About 1870, Miles Dent floated his last raft down the Bennett's Branch.

RAFTERS – LOGGER WAR

A picture of a steam driven sawmill on the Bennett's Branch.
Picture was from a collection of Dents Run Pictures

Many serious problems between the loggers and raftsmen occurred when loggers began floating logs down the Susquehanna to Williamsport. A shooting war broke out on the West Branch known as the logger and raftsman war in 1857. This matter was soon resolved, more to the benefit of the loggers than the rafters, but logging did have a serious impact on the rafting of pine spars. However, in the early 1860's, the Civil War created a strong demand for oak spars which pumped new life into the rafting of spar logs. Prior to 1860, 10% or less of the spars was oak, but after this date a raft consisted of 50 to 90% oak spars. Because of the heavy density of the oak spars, a certain amount of light weight pine spars were needed to float the raft.

A PRUDENT EMPLOYER

Dent was a hardworking, prudent man who believed in leading by example. He would never ask his men to do anything he wouldn't or couldn't do. He paid his men the prevailing wage and believed in an honest day's pay for an honest day's work. Wood hicks were generally paid by the day and were provided room and board while working out of camp for both paid days and non paid days which normally included Sundays and rain days. Someone told Tom, one of Dent's hands that if hired out "wet and dry", he would be paid for wet days. This appealed to Tom, and he asked Dent about working on the wet and dry schedule.

"So you want to work wet and dry, do you?" asked Dent.

"Yes, I do, Mr. Dent," replied Tom.

"All right, I will see that you work that way." said Dent

Dent took Tom with him to fix the road. A steady rain set in. The teams and helpers went to camp, but Dent kept right on fixing the road. It kept right on raining, and Tom was getting wetter and wetter until he finally said to Dent: "Mr. Dent, it not too wet to work?"

"Not a bit of it," replied Dent.

"But the teams and all the other men have gone to camp. Why do we stay out in the rain?" asked Tom

Dent replied, "Did you not hire to work wet or dry?"

"Yes, but this is all wet," replied Tom

"You expect your pay," said Dent. "You cannot get pay that you do not earn."

"Well, Mr. Dent, I do not like this kind of a deal. What can I do?" asked Tom.

"Do as other men do. Work on dry days and get paid. Lie in on wet days and get your board," replied Dent.

"I see you point, Mr. Dent," said Tom. "I think it is well taken and I will be satisfied to work the customary way."

CAMP MENU

A lumber camp menu for the wood hicks would typically consist of wheat and corn bread, corn mush, molasses cake, griddle cakes, potatoes, turnips, sauer-kraut, beans, dried corn and rice, smoked ham, corn beef, salt pork, salt fish, fresh beef, and pork. During the cold weather, molasses, honey, sugar, prunes, and dried apples were added. In the summer months they had the luxury of eggs, milk, and fresh fruit. On occasion wild game would be part of the menu. One winter day a deer was killed and put on top of the camp building to freeze. During that night an animal crawled on top of the building and ate some of the deer. The entire crew was curious as to what sort of critter had chewed on their future dinner. Most of the men thought it was a panther, as panthers were reported in the Dent's Run area at the time. A strong trap was placed near the back corner of the camp where this mysterious critter had crawled up on the roof. The next morning a very large bobcat was caught in the trap. The cat weighted forty-three pounds.

The quality of food in most logging camps depended more on the cookie than the food. In some of the smaller camp the wood hicks would take turns doing the cooking. As one story goes, a rule that many smaller logging camps had was that the last person who complained about the food was the next camp cook. Charlie had been cooking for quite a spell, and he yearned to give up his cooking duties and return to the woods to work. So one evening he put an excessive amount of salt in the beans. The first hick who gulped down a large spoonful of beans cried out, "God, these beans are salty", but realizing what he had said, he quickly added, "But its just the way I like them." Obviously he didn't want to be the next cook. As the quality of food varied from camp to camp, the logger had a secret code. They would bury an axe head near the entrance of a camp. If the axe head was buried upside down it indicated the food in this camp was bad. This would warn newcomers as to the quality of the camp food.

THE CAMP BULLY

Fighting in logging camps amongst the hicks was a common and frequent occurrence to settle various camp quarrels, and it provided entertainment for the crew. Most logging camps had a mix of many different nationalities, and differences on both religious and political views, would on many occasions create sparks that would often develop into a rip roaring fire. Generally these fights did not occur in camp, but in the neighboring town(s), quite often starting in a bar room. However, there would be camp challenges now and then that would take place in camp. An example would be if one hick took another hick's seat in the mess hall. When this occurred, quite often the hick who lost the fight would leave camp for another job.

Almost every camp had a camp bully. This person would frequently provoke a fight, often with a camp greenhorn, to prove that he was the champion fighter, or alpha hick in the camp. These fighting ruffians on the Sinnemahoning would go out of their way to challenge and fight anyone with a tough man reputation, for the sole purpose of claiming the title of Champion or King of the fighting men. In most cases these fights would be a one round fight, and the winner was generally the last one standing, or until one of them gave up. Fighting had no rules – kicking, gouging, elbowing, and biting, whatever it took to win. "Getting the leathers put to you" was a logger's term for getting kicked by a corked foot.

COMES A CHALLENGE

Stories about Dent carrying the railroad frog as easily as an ordinary man could carry a small sack of flour spread up and down the Sinnemahoning Rive like a wild fire.

Tim Crone bragged that he was the King Fighter on the banks of Sinnemahoning. He boasted of beating nearly all the best fighting men on the river. When Crone heard these wild tales about Dent, he decided to pay him a visit and challenge him to a fight. When Crone arrived at Dents Run, Dent was plowing a field across the creek from his house with a yoke of oxen. Crone approached Dent just as he was unhitching the oxen from the plow to go to dinner. Crone, not knowing this farmer, asked him, "Do you know where Miles Dent lives?" Dent calmly picked up the plow by the handles, pointed it towards his house, and said, "He lives right over yonder in that house on the hill side." Still holding the plow as a pointer towards his house, Dent watched as Crone mumbled a "thank you" and walked away.

CRONE KING OF THE RIVER?

That evening while Crone was having dinner at a local saloon, he was bragging to the bartender about all the fighting men he had beaten from here to Lock Haven. "I have come a long way to challenge Dent to a fight," said Crone.

The bartender grinned and said, "You might be opening up a can of worms you don't want to eat. Dent is so strong that he can twist your head off your shoulders quicker than a wink."

"Yea, but I think I can bring Dent to his knees", Crone replied.

"You know," the bartender said, " that another man like you just a short while ago came here with the same idea. Just like you he came all the way from Lock Haven to fight Dent. He encountered Dent driving down towards Hick Run in his oxen drawn wagon. 'You Miles Dent?' the stranger asked.

To which Dent replied, 'yes I am, how can I help you?' '

I came here to challenge you to a fight', said the stranger.

Dent got down off the wagon and grabbed the dude by the back of the neck with his left hand, holding him at arms- length, while flaying him with an ox whip he had in his right hand. The big fellow dangled in the air, begging and pleading for Dent to put him down.

'Now', said Dent, 'You go back to Lock Haven and tell all ruffians you know about Miles Dent, and that he is not a fighting man'."

I surprised you never heard of that encounter", the bartender continued, "and let me tell you, when that stranger's feet hit the ground running, he ran all the way back to Lock Haven.

Crone, obviously still vividly remembering how Dent had picked up the plow like a stick, and more than likely aware of the stranger's prior encounter with the whip, apparently decided he couldn't lose to a person he had never fought and returned home.

DENTS RUN THE TOWN

Sometime in 1860's Miles Dent laid out a plot for the village of Dents Run which included both residential and commercial lots. In 1865, he built a grist mill, and the following year he a built small water-powered saw mill, thus providing the village with both flour and saw boards. A copy of Dent's plan was filed and is recorded at the Elk Court House in Ridgway.

THE DENTS RUN CHURCH

DENTS RUN SCHOOL HOUSE
Picture courtesy of the Harrison

Dent built a community building for citizens of Dents Run. One day a young traveling preacher approached Miles and asked him if he could use the building for a prayer meeting. Miles told the preacher that if his services would benefit the citizens of the community, he could use the church free of charge. The young preacher, anxious to win over converts, asked Mr. Dent if he belonged to the church. Dent was quick to inform the preacher in an authoritarian tone "Belong? Heck, I own the church."

THE RIP-SNORTING BULL

In developing the village of Dents Run, Miles was always looking for ways to improve the quality of life in the community. One of the problems, Dent determined, was that the inferior breed of local milk cows produced a poor quality of cream used in making butter. Dents solution was simple; he purchased a big Jersey Bull to upgrade the breed of the local cows. In the early days, cows, horses, pigs and other domestic animals roamed freely. A common old saying was that a good fence was "hog tight, bull strong, and horse high."

Dent's big bull roamed freely throughout the village and frequently would wander up to the neighboring village of Grant. One Sunday afternoon several mischievous teenagers decided to have a little fun, and at the same time get rid of this troublesome animal for once and all. The boys enticed the bull into a barn with the aid of a little hay, and while the bull munched on the hay, they tied a big brass cowbell securely to the end of his tail. They then pointed the bull towards Dents Run, and with the aid of a switch, sent the bull running home. The big bull took off running down the road just a snorting and bellowing, obviously frightened by the sound of the bell. The faster he ran the louder the bell rang, and the louder the bell rang the faster the raging bull raced down through the valley with the bell bouncing on and off his back. The frantic bull didn't stop at home; he tore through the village of Dents Run, bucking and kicking like the mad hysterical creature he was and headed down to Hicks Run. Miles was sitting on his porch, overlooking the valley, when the bull came tearing by, and would later say it was a laughable show. Somewhere in all this commotion, the bell got caught between some saplings and tore loose from the bull's tail, and eventually the big bull returned home with his tail between his legs. However, his fate was doomed. Miles, not wanting his stock tearing up the neighbor's property, butchered the poor bull. Miles never again purchased another community bull.

THE BUSINESS MAN

ISAIAH DENT
Picture courtesy of Shirley Harrison

In the 1870's, Dent owned and operated a store in Benezette, which his oldest son, Isaiah, managed for a number of years. The store was a profitable venture. In 1881, Dent built a steam operated sawmill at Dents Run, with a daily capacity of 30,000 board feet. This mill was the most modern mill of its kind on the Bennett's Branch in its era.

SUPER NATURAL STRENGTH

The citizens of Benezette were milling around the polling house on Election Day in 1872, which pitted U. S. Grant against Horace Greeley. Miles Dent, a leading Democrat, and Erasmus Morey were arguing about the outcome of the election. A huge fly wheel that weighed about thirteen hundred pounds was sitting by the railroad depot near the polling house. Morey claimed that Greeley didn't have anymore of a chance of getting elected president than Miles Dent had of lifting the huge fly wheel, and offered free drinks to the crowd if he could. Dent walked over to the wheel and straddled the hub; bending down over the wheel, he firmly took a spoke in each hand. As he straightened up, the huge fly wheel cleared the ground. Dent, dropping the wheel to the ground, turned to Morey saying, "You will have to bet again".

MAN OF INFULUNCE

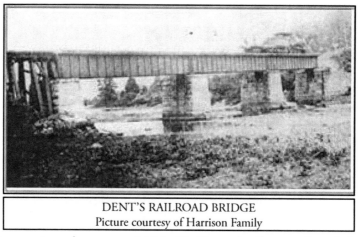

DENT'S RAILROAD BRIDGE
Picture courtesy of Harrison Family

Some time between 1883-85 Dent built a railroad bridge across the Bennett's Branch to accommodate the railroad he built up Dents Run Valley. An undocumented story claims that when the construction of the bridge was completed, the political powers of the day discovered the abutment(s) on the south side of the branch had crossed the county line which was not on Dent's property. Dent, a man of influence, to solve this problem had the county line moved. The bridge abutments are still visible today, as well as the jog in the county line. Many tons of coal were hauled across this bridge from the mines in Wilmer.

Miles and Lydia Miller Dent reared eight children: Isaiah, Hiram, Flilancy, Austin, Alice Cecile - (Mrs. S. S. Billings), Warren, Abel, Mary Emily (Mrs. John R. Hicks), and Rachel. Lydia died December 1897, Miles on March 18, 1899, at the age of 76. They are buried in the Hick Run Cemetery.

Miles Dent was the son of one the earliest Pioneer settlers on the Bennett's Branch. He began life with a limited education and without any social advantages. He was a hard working, law abiding, family man who constantly strove to improve the general welfare of the area citizens. He was one of the first to put pine spars on the Bennett's Branch. He was known as a prominent lumberman throughout the Commonwealth. He was a successful merchant farmer, a man of many talents with extra physical strength. The Paul Bunyan of the Bennett's Branch, Miles Dent was a man whose deeds and accomplishments have made him a legend for the centuries.

THE END

1. History of McKean, Elk, Cameron and Potter Counties Penna., Vol 1 – J.H. Beers.
2. A Story of the Sinnamahone by George William Huntley, Jr.
3. .Looking for Ephraim by Helen Dixon Huges
4. .Elk County Deomocrat.
5. My Pardner, The River - Tonkin

THE MIX FAMILY

Amos Mix and his wife Clarinda were among the very first settlers on the Bennett's Branch, coming to the Valley about 1812. Amos and his family settled near the mouth of a tributary of the branch located between Dents Run and Driftwood that would eventually bear his name – Mix Run, obviously named after Amos and his family. This would be the birthplace of the famous cowboy movie star Tom Mix, the flamboyant descendant of Amos and Clarinda.

TOM AND HIS MOTHER,
ELIZABETH SMITH MIX

Thomas Mix immigrated to New Haven, Connecticut, about 1640, and is the first known ancestor of Amos Mix to set foot in America. Thomas, son of Daniel Meekes, was born sometime between 1624 and 1629 in London, Middlesex, England. It appears that shortly after his arrival here the name Mix evolved from Meekes. Thomas's name appears on a list in London as being among the first grantees of land in New Haven. New Haven was officially formed in 1639, and Thomas was a very early resident of the Colony.

After arriving at New Haven, Thomas was attracted to a young, beautiful girl by the name of Rebecca Turner. It would appear by all accounts that a love affair developed between the two. However, Rebecca's father was not fond of the young Mix as a suitable suitor for his lovely and rich daughter. Rebecca's father,

Captain Nathaniel Turner, came to America about 1630 and was a well-respected citizen of the New English Colony. He had gained a reputation as a brave and distinguished soldier, having led a successful expedition against the Pequot Indians. Captain Turner later served as Chief Military Officer and Deputy to the English Court of Combination and was elected as magistrate of the New Haven Colony. He was also a wealthy and successful planter.

Thomas had a great deal of respect for the Captain, and perhaps this was part of his attraction to Rebecca. However, the Captain considered Mix to be a headstrong, obstinate young man, who was an unwelcome annoyance to the welfare of the colony. It was obvious that the Captain did not want his daughter involved with Thomas.

Fate intervened. In 1646, the Captain's position as Deputy to the English Courts of Combination required him to return to England. Both he and the ship he was sailing on, the *Phantom* were lost at sea. Three years later in 1649, his widow married Samuel Goodendausen, and the sweethearts Thomas and Rebecca were married as a matter of necessity as evidenced by following 1649 New Haven court records:

Thomas Meekes and Rebecca Turner were called before ye court to answer to their sinful miscaring in matter of fornication with sundry lyes added thereto by them both in grose and hainiouse manner. The matter having bine formerly heard before the gouerner in a private way, wch was now declared to ye court in ther prsenc, and they called to answer. Thomas Meekes said he could say nothing against whath bine declared but it is true, and he desires to judge and condeme himself for it in ye sight of God and his people. And for Rebecca Turner, she ackknowledg the things ye charged was true, and thought she had saide Thomas Meekes had to do with her but once, yet it was oftener, as she now saith.

Thomas and Rebecca would experience some minor legal encounters in their younger years, but as the years went on Tom became a successful member of the colony and served as constable. Captain Turner would have been proud to see this young rebel do well. Seven of Thomas and Rebecca's children were early graduates of Yale. Thomas and Rebecca sired ten children: John, Nathaniel, Daniel, Thomas, Rebecca, Abigail, Caleb, Samuel, Hannah, Esther, and Stephen.

Thomas died in 1692 in New Haven and was buried on the "Green" of this city. His estate at this time was considered substantial and was divided among his children. Rebecca lived to a ripe old age, passing on in 1731.

From Thomas to Amos Mix there are five generations:

Daniel Mix born New Haven, Conn. – married Ruth Rockwell, his son

Thomas Mix born New Haven, Conn. – married Deborah Royce, his son

Josiah Mix born New Haven, Conn. – married Sybil Holt/ Abigail Porter

Eldad Mix born New Haven, Conn. – married Lydia Beach

Amos Mix was born on February 2, 1759, in New Haven, Connecticut, the son of Eldad and Lydia Beach Mix. On January 4, 1784 Amos married Clarinda Barner in New Haven. They had three children: Hannah Louisa, James, and Levi. The father, Eldad was a veteran of the French and Indian War and served in Connecticut 2nd Reg, 7th Co. under the command of Col. Nathan Whiting. Amos was a veteran of Revolutionary War and served as a private in the 4th Reg., under Col. Butler.

Amos Mix has a number of interesting, if somewhat distant, family relationships:

Robert Morris who was instrumental in purchasing most of the land west of the Alleganies in Pa. from the Seneca Indians, and who helped George Washington finance the Revolutionary War was a distant grandson.

Francis Lightfoot Lee was a 4th cousin 1 time removed. Lee was a general under George Washington in the Revolutionary War, and father of General Robert E. Lee.

Millard Fillmore – 13th President of the United States was a 4th cousin 1 time removed.

Samuel Morse – American Inventor was a 5th cousin.

Rutherford B. Hayes 19th President of United States was a 4th cousin 2 times removed.

First Lady Helen Taft was a 4th cousin 3 times removed

John Wayne, American actor was a 4th cousin 4 time removed.

Robert Frost - American poet was a 5th cousin 2 times removed

First Lady Julia Tyler was a 6th cousin 1 time removed.

Humphrey Bogart - American actor was a 5th cousin 3 time removed

Walt Disney was a 5th cousin 3 time removed

Florence Nightingale was a 7th cousin

Ralph Waldo Emerson - American Author was a 4th cousin.

Eli Whitney was a 3rd Cousin 1 time removed.

Oliver Wendell Homes was a 4th cousin 1 time removed.

First Lady Lucy Webb Hayes was a 4th cousin 2 time removed.

Frank Lloyd Wright was a 5th cousin 4 times removed

First Lady Jacqueline Kennedy was a 4th cousin 5 times removed.

President Gerald Ford was a 4th cousin 4 times removed

Gregory Peck was a 4th cousin 5 times removed

Alfred Tennyson - English Poet was a 7th cousin.

President John F. Kennedy was a 4th cousin 6 times removed.

According to Erasmus Morey who referred to his father's notes of the time when the Moreys came to the Bennett's Valley to settle in April of 1813 – he writes:

"But on our 8th day of traveling with a raw crew, the boats lay on Sugar Creek bottom near where Robert Smith lives."

"The party camped in the woods at night and it was very rainy. We arrived at Rogers' cabin, the families and boatmen and everyone else much fatigued. The cabin was 16' x 20' and one can imagine that this last arrival of guests filled the small cabin to its utmost capacity, as living already with Dr. Rogers was the AMOS MIX family.

Elias Edwin Mix was born on November 8, 1853 in Mix Run, the son of Solomon, great grandson of Amos, and Lorahama Barr Mix. Elias's occupation was a lumberman, contract hauler for the local mills, and later in life, a caretaker for John E. Du Bois's stables. Mr. Mix was called Ed, or sometimes Edward, by the people who knew him. In 1875, he married Elizabeth Smith from Lancaster. Edward lived in a small wood framed house, located in Mix Run on ½ acre of property given to them by Rev. Thomas Hollen. Edward and Elizabeth had four children: Tom, Harry, Emma (Mrs. Swartz), and Ester who was the wife of Dr. Bell.

Tom Mix, the Cowboy Movie Star

Tom was born in Mix Run on January 6, 1880. As a young lad growing up, his mother would often describe Tom as not a bad boy, but very mischievous, and in his films, he was invariably on the right side of things. She went on to tell a story that on one occasion, upon returning home from a trip, she found Tom had stretched her best linen tablecloth against the wall and was throwing knives at it. Naturally she was upset, but what alarmed her most was that he had his little sister standing in front of the tablecloth while Tom was trying to stick knives around her. She told of another incident when Tom was sent to the pasture to bring in the cows. A little later she looked out the window and saw Tom returning in a downpour of rain, riding one of the cows while holding an umbrella over his head.

Edward and his family moved from Mix Run to Driftwood when Tom was about three years old. They lived in Driftwood for a short time and then moved to Du Bois, where Edward became a caretaker for John E. Du Bois's stables. It is strongly assumed that while here Tom learned a good deal about horsemanship from his father.

Following Tom's tour of duty with the army, he went west and spent a few years living and working on ranches, four years of which were spent on the famous Miller Brothers 101 Ranch. In Texas, Tom became a real life cowboy. He refined his horsemanship skills and became a rodeo champion. Tom was an expert marksman with both a rifle and pistol, to the degree that he could perform shooting exhibitions. In addition to these skills, he was an accomplished roper, and later in life he would perform on stage with the famous Will Rogers. Mix and Wyatt Earp were close friends, and when Wyatt died, Tom was a pallbearer at his funeral. Witnesses claim that Mix wept at Wyatt Earp's passing.

Tom Mix, like his ancestor Amos Mix before him, who was a pioneer settler on the Bennett's Branch, was a pioneer in his own right. Tom was a pathfinder in the film industry in the early development of Western movies. He blazed a trail in this industry that many famous Western film stars would follow. .

Tom was unique in that he was a cowboy turned movie star, and when he got the opportunity to act, he became a world famous actor and performer. Tom performed his own stunts, and had many broken bones to prove his death defying acts.

From 1910 to 1935 Tom Mix made over 350 movies of which only six were talkies. These early films grossed over an amazing six million dollars. Nearing the end of his career, Tom had a traveling road show that included performances in Europe and Austria. It has been rumored that on one occasion his show came to Du Bois, and at this show he refused to acknowledge his mother who was in the audience, as he desired to be recognized by the public as a true Texas cowboy. True or false, this has never been verified. However, in an interview late in life, Tom was asked where he was born. His answer was Texas. Another story promoted about Tom Mix was that his mother was half Indian. Elizabeth, his mother, would become very upset when she read about or heard untrue statements about her son Tom, and she never hesitated to set the record straight, especially on statements regarding his birth place or ancestry.

On October 12, 1940, Tom Mix died in an automobile accident when the 1937 Cord he was driving plunged into a ravine. The ravine was later named "The Tom Mix Wash" in his honor. A roadside memorial at the site of this accident reads:

TOM MIX – January 6, 1880 – October 12, 1940 whose spirit left his body

On this spot and whose characterization and portrayals in life served

To better fix memories of the old west in the minds of living men.

At the dedication of this memorial, his friend Gene Autry, who was also a pallbearer at his funeral, sang "Empty Saddles" as a tribute to his accomplishments.

THE END
Tom Mix heavily Illustrated Biography with Raphy – Tom E. Mix
King Cowboy Tom Mix & Movie – Robert S. Birchard.
History of McKean, Elk, Cameron and Potter Counties – Beers
Johnson Family History – Eva J. Caylor
Mix History by Sylvia E. Wilkinson

THE WINSLOWS

Picture of performer playing the role of Edward Winslow at Plimoth Plantation in Plymouth, Massachusetts. Picture by James Burke.

In the early 14th century in England the Winslow family emerged as a loosely knit clan living in the vicinity of the hamlet of Winslow in Burkinghamshire, from which they adopted their name WINSLOW. Burkinghamshire is located about 50 miles northwest of London. Five Winslow brothers: Edward, John, Josiah, Gilbert, and Kenelm, all sons of Edward and Magdalene Oliver Winslow, migrated to America beginning with the *Mayflower's* maiden voyage to Plymouth in 1620. One brother, Gilbert, would return to England (home) on the *Mayflower,* while the other four brothers would distinguish themselves as early American settlers.

The Winslow's early footprints upon this land are lasting tracks in the annals of early American History. From Edward Winslow's arrival on the *Mayflower* as a member of the Plymouth Colony in 1620, to Reuben Winslow's founding of Benezette in the1840's and beyond, the Winslows have a rich family tradition spanning over two hundred years in the pioneering heritage of this country.

The Mayflower 1620

Edward Winslow was among the 102 Pilgrims who came to America on the *Mayflower*. Edward played a very important role in the leadership and development of the Plymouth Colony. In 1621, he negotiated in a treaty of Peace and Friendship with the Indian Chief Massasoit. Edward returned to England in 1623-1624 as an agent of the Colony, and while he was in England he wrote "Good News from England," later published in 1625 by Samuel Purchas. On his return to Plymouth, he was elected an Assistant of the Colony and was continuously re-elected until 1647, with the exception of the three years he served as governor in1633-1634 and 1644-1645. Edward was the first person to introduce cattle to New England. He and his bovines came on a return trip from England. Edward is acknowledged as the first Englishman to explore Connecticut. In addition to his other accomplishments at the Plymouth Colony, Edward was instrumental in negotiating a discharge of the Plymouth Colony's debts owed to their English backers.

Plymouth Serrated Cupboard believed to be crafted by Kenelm Winslow.

Kenelm Winslow, the ancestor to the Winslows who eventually became the founders of Benezette, was born in Droitwich, England, on April 29, 1599. At an early age, Kenelm migrated from England to Holland with an apprenticeship as a joiner. A joiner is a skilled carpenter or wood craftsman capable of mortising, tenoning, dovetailing, woodcarving and having knowledge and skill to the intricacies of assembling these items into exquisite wood furniture.

Kenelm came to Plymouth on the *Mayflower's* second voyage to America in 1629. Upon arriving in Plymouth he became a "freeman" which gave him the right to vote and own land in the Colony. Although Kenelm could own land, not being a "first comer", he was not included in the division of land. In June of 1634, Kenelm married Ellen (Eleanor) Newton

Adams, a widow of John Adams who arrived at Plymouth in 1621 on the ship Fortune.

Here in Plymouth, Kenelm renewed his profession as a joiner and became the second joiner in the Plymouth Colony. On January 6, 1633-34, Samuel Jenny, son of John Jenny, was apprenticed to Kenelm as a joiner for four years. John Alden, a founder, was considered as the Colony's first joiner. Unlike Kenelm, Alden had no former training as a joiner. He was hired by the Pilgrims as a cooper, or barrel maker, for the Mayflower's voyage to America. He joined the Plymouth Colony and rose from his common seaman status to become a prominent member of the Colony. John Alden, for you who remember your early American History, was the subject of Henry Wadsworth Longfellow in The Courtship of Miles Standish. Longfellow alleged that Miles Standish asked John Alden to ask Priscilla Mullens on his behalf for her hand in marriage. When Alden popped the question, Priscilla told him. "Why don't you speak for yourself John"? Whether or not this story is true, John and Priscilla did become husband and wife.

Kenelm's skill and expertise as a joiner in crafting exquisite and eloquent wood furniture pieces such as cupboards, chests, and tables would become legendary and establish a seventeenth century tradition in wood furniture that would create a Plymouth Colony legacy. Many of Kenelm's pieces were custom made for notable people of the day, which gives each of these pieces a particular historical significance. Some of the furniture that Kenelm made is still in existence today. A Plymouth Serrated Cupboard believed to be crafted by Kenelm is on exhibit at the Metropolitan Museum of Art in New York City.

About 1641, Kenelm moved to Marshfield, then called Green Harbor, having previously received on March 5, 1637-38, a grant for a parcel of land there. The grant was from Josiah Winslow, his brother, to both him and Love Brewster, conditioned upon Kenelm's portion of land adjoining his brother's land and that the lands be settled upon. The grant described the land as a parcel remaining of that neck of land lying on the east side of the lands lately granted to Josiah Winslow.

Miss Thomas, in her memories of Marshfield, said that Kenelm settled on a gentle eminence by the sea, near the extremity of a neck of land lying between Green Harbor and South Rivers. This tract of the township was considered the Eden of the region. It was beautified with groves of majestic oaks and graceful walnuts, with an understory devoid of tangled shrubbery.

Edward Winslow is the acknowledged founder of Marshfield, and here in Marshfield he established the first church, the first school, and organized the first town meeting. The Winslow settlement soon had a road, which could well be the first official road in the country. Parts of this road, known today as the Pilgrim Trail, still exist. In 1841, Kenelm was elected as the Colony's surveyor. During his tenure as surveyor he was fined. It is not certain if the fine was for the Pilgrim Trail but a story survives that Kenelm was fined 10 shillings for riding his horse on the Sabbath.

The Kenelm Winslow House dated 1645 still stands in Marshfield. This house is currently owned (2007) by Mr. & Mrs.

Kenelm Winslow's house in Marshfield, Massachusetts now owned by Mr. Mrs. Frank Farrell.

Frank Farrell, located on 123 Winslow Road. The Farrells have done extensive remodeling to the old Winslow house but have retained the look of the original exterior to preserve its historical heritage. The remolded interior presents a very attractive and comfortable home.

Frank Farrell, a retired Chief Petty Officer, when giving the author a private tour of his home, explained the house has a white chimney, with a black cap, signifying to passers by that this was the home of Separatists. The Pilgrims were English Separatists who broke away from the Church of England because they felt that the church had not completed the work of the Reformation. Mr. Farrell, while showing the main fireplace, went on to explain that this was where both the cooking and laundry were done in early times. He pointed to the large cooking pot and went on to mention the origin of the old fable, "Who put the overhauls in Mrs. Murphy's soup".

On June 4, 1645, Kenelm appealed a decision of the Colony Court (Bench) in a case involving one John Maynard. The committee, which included Myles Standish, upheld the Bench's ruling, and the court ordered Kenelm to be imprisoned and fined 10 pounds. Upon Kenelm's petition filed that same day, he acknowledged his offense and sorrow for the same. The Bench amended their verdict, released Kenelm from imprisonment, and suspended his fine for one year, on condition that if he showed good behavior over that period, the fine would be rescinded.

Kenelm, over the years, acquired a number of parcels of land that he either received as a grant or purchased. Kenelm's brothers Gilbert and Edward came to Plymouth on the Mayflower in 1620. Although Gilbert was under twenty-one when he signed the Mayflower Compact and returned to England shortly after his arrival here, he was considered a "first comer" and included in the colony's division of land. When Gilbert died in England, Kenelm and his brother John inherited Gilbert's land grant in Plymouth. Kenelm was also one of the twenty-six original proprietors of

Assonet (Freetown), Mass., which was purchased from the Indians on April 2, 1659. Kenelm received the 24th lot.

Nathaniel, Kenelm's second son, inherited the homestead, and upon his death, it passed into the hands of his son, Kenelm who married Abigail Waterman, then to their son Kenelm, who married Abigail Bourne, The latter Kenelm was obliged to sell the place in consequence of the failure in business of his younger brother Joseph.

Kenelm married Eleanor Adams in June of 1634, widow of John Adams, of Plymouth. She survived him and died at Marshfield, Mass., at the age of 83 where she was buried December 5, 1681. Kenelm died on September 13, 1672, at the age of seventy-three in Salem, Mass., where he had gone on business. According to Rev. L. R. Paige, he died there apparently after a long sickness. In his will dated five weeks earlier, 8 Aug, 1672, he describes himself as being very sick and drawing nigh unto death. He may have been in Salem to visit his niece Mrs. Elizabeth Corwin, daughter of his brother Edward Winslow, or perhaps he went to Salem to obtain medical aid.

Winslow monument in the Winslow cemetery in Marshfield.

In the Winslow cemetery in Marshfield, there is a monument honoring Edward, his wife Susana, Kenelm and his wife Ellen, Josiah and his wife Penelope, along with other Winslows. Edward died and was buried at sea. Located just a few yards from the Winslow Monument is the gravesite of Daniel Webster.

Daniel Webster, as most history buffs know, was a famous American attorney, United States Senator and Secretary of State to three Presidents. Sometime in the 1800's Webster purchased the Isaac Winslow house in Marshfield. Isaac built this house in 1699 on land that was granted to his grandfather Edward Winslow in the 1630s. Today this historic house serves as a Winslow museum and hosts a variety of functions which include the Winslow family reunions.

Kenelm was a Puritan pioneer of North America, a master joiner, land owner, farmer, and a part time ship builder who obtained the position of Deputy in the General Court from 1642 to 44 and from 1649 to 53. He also served a number of minor offices in the Colony. He married Eleanor Newton Adams, and together they raised four children: Job, Kenelm, Nathaniel, and Elinor.

JOB WINSLOW & RUTH CHASE COLE
SECOND GENERATION

Job Winslow, Kenelm's son, was born about 1641. Around 1666, he settled at Swansey, Massachusetts, located about 48 miles south of Boston. Here Job Winslow lived for about nine years and was living in Swansey when the King Philip War erupted in June of 1675. This war, according to most historians, was the bloodiest war in American history. The war pitted Metacom (called King Philip by the English, sachem of the Wampanoag) allied with the Narragansett, against the colonists allied with several Indian tribes including the Pequots, Mohegans and Niantics. The war quickly spread throughout the New England area with a dreadful outcome. Over 90 settlements in the region were attacked and more than a dozen villages were totally destroyed including Brookfield, Deerfield and Northfield. One in ten soldiers on both sides was injured or killed. There were about 600 settlers and over 3000 Indians killed. The war proved devastating for the colonists and fatal for the Indians.

The cause of the war was primarily the colonists' hunger for land and their heavy handed treatment of the Wampanoag. One incident that angered Metacom and his people, the Wampanoag, happened in 1662, when Josiah Winslow, Job's uncle, acting on behalf of the Plymouth Colony, captured Wamsutta, Metacom's brother at gun point for questioning. Soon after his interrogation

Wamsutta died. This sudden death and interrogation angered Metacom (the Wampanoag) which caused a breakdown of relations that led to war.

In any event, when war broke out in Swansey, nine settlers were killed and Job's home was burnt down. It appears from various records that Job relocated at Rochester, and then sometime about 1686 he moved to Freetown. Located on the banks of the Assonet River, Freetown was first settled on April 2, 1659 when the areas of the Assonet and Fall River were purchased from the Wampanoag Indians in an exchange known as Ye Freemen's Purchase. The town was officially incorporated in July 1683 as part of the Plymouth Colony. In 1685, the Plymouth Colony merged with Massachusetts Bay Colony.

In Freetown, Job became a distinguished man both in political and religious matters which were quite entangled at the time. He was a selectman and in 1690 a Town Clerk and grand juryman. In 1691, 1701-1706 and 1711, Job was the assessor of Freetown. In 1708 and 1711, he was moderator of the annual town meetings. In 1686, Job was deputy to the General Court, and in 1692 served at the first General Court in Massachusetts under the charter of William and Mary.

Job held the rank of Lieutenant, probably in the Freetown Militia. His main occupation and source of income was as a shipwright.

Job married Ruth Chase Cole. They had thirteen children, son James being the ancestor of the Benezette Winslows. Job died July 14, 1720. In his will dated November 12, 1717, he donated the lot known as the Winslow Burying Ground, located two miles south of Assonet Village.

JAMES WINSLOW & ELIZABETH CARPENTER
THIRD GENERATION

James, Kenelm's grandson, the eventual grandfather of Carpenter, was born on May 9, 1687, in Freetown, Bristol, Mass.

He married Elizabeth Carpenter on 1708 in Freetown. James was the first of the Winslows to move to what is now Maine. He obtained a land grant and in Falmouth he built a mill. At this time, a large part of Maine and Kennebec County was within the limits of the grant of the old "Plymouth Council" to William Bradford in 1629. James and Elizabeth had seven children with his son James being the oldest.

JAMES WINSLOW & ANNA HUSTON
FOURTH GENERATION

James, Carpenter's father, was born August 6, 1725, in Freetown, Bristol, Mass. James and his brothers who lived in Portland received a large tract of land from their father in Broad Bay Maine and moved there in 1752. Indian troubles forced them to move to the Pittston area as one of the first settlers in the fall of 1760. His wife Anna and daughter Sarah were the first white females in Pittston. His son Jonathon was the first white child born there on March 23, 1761. The Winslows and McCauslands built a log cottage, which they occupied together. James Winslow as a young man was a drummer in the fort at Falmouth. Sometime later, he converted to the Society of Friends, a group that abhorred all aspects of war. James refused to serve in the Revolution because of his Quaker principles.

However, he did make 50 paddles for Benedict Arnold's expedition. During the Revolution the family relocated to the back of their farm to avoid detection from British soldiers whom they worried might come into the area. Anna "Granny" (McCausland) Huston Winslow, a very energetic woman, was the only physician for the early settlers until 1769. James was a millwright and very early became familiar with the use of mechanical shipbuilding and had a shipyard at Wiscasset, Maine, for several years. James and Anna had one son Carpenter.

CARPENTER & ELIZABETH COLE WINSLOW
FIFTH GENERATION

Carpenter Winslow was born in Pittston, Maine, on March 22, 1766. He married Elizabeth Colburn, the daughter of Major Ruben and Elizabeth Colburn. The Major lived at the time of the Arnold Expedition and took an active part in the American Revolution. Elizabeth was of Huguenot ancestry.

According to *The History of Jefferson County*, "In 1815, Carpenter Winslow brought his family to Jefferson County. It is said he first made a temporary location in Clearfield County in 1819, at which time he purchased his farm in what is now Gaskill Township, Jefferson County, and after erecting buildings he settled there in the year 1821. His family was the first family to settle in what is now Gaskill Township."

It was reported that R.C. Winslow claimed, when speaking of the Winslow Ancestry, at a Winslow reunion in 1908 at Benezette, that Carpenter Winslow Sr. and family moved to Pennsylvania around 1815. R.C. went on to say that they came up the Susquehanna River to Clearfield by building a bridge across the river. Then they went down the Wilderness Road to Punxsutawney and became crop farmers.

According to public records, Carpenter's son, Carpenter, and his wife Beulah's second child George Wait Winslow born on May 25, 1820, in Maine, while their third child Ebenezer was born on April 12, 1823, in Jefferson County, Pennsylvania.

The census indicates that Carpenter and his family were living in Perry Township, Jefferson County in 1820. Gaskill Township would later, after the Winslow's arrival here, be carved from Perry Township.

In 1819, Benezette was located in Clearfield County, and some accounts claim that the family lived there for about a year before moving on to Jefferson County.

The dates indicated in the above information pertaining to Carpenter and his family's arrival to the Bennett's Branch, and then on to Jefferson, is somewhat confusing to say the least.

To approach these dates logically, it appears that Carpenter and several of his boys came up the Bennett's Branch sometime between 1815 to 1818, and took up temporary residency about a mile below the current town off Benezette. In 1819, Carpenter purchased land in what is now Gaskill Township, Jefferson County, and here he began carving out a home in the wildness, clearing the land for a farm and erecting buildings. It would further appear that sometime between 1820 and 1823, that Carpenter may have returned to Maine and brought the remaining members of his family to their new home in Jefferson County.

In any event, the Carpenter Winslow family journey began by sailing from Maine to Baltimore, and then from Baltimore they came up the Susquehanna River to Lock Haven. The last leg of their journey was a two and half day canoe trip up the river to settle about one mile east of the present day village of Benezette. Here they lived for about a year.

The country then was a dense wilderness, and like all new settlers the Winslows experienced many hardships in their struggle to carve out an existence in this land. They found the soil very productive for planting, but hard to clear. Fortunately, the surrounding forest and streams provided abundant wild game and fish to supplement their meager diet.

Carpenter died in November 1827; his wife, Elizabeth, survived by about 18 years. They are buried in the old Findley Street Cemetery in Punxsutawney, Penna.

That same year, 1827, his sons Reuben, Ebenezer, and Carpenter purchased from Leonard Morey 379 ½ acres of land near the mouth of Trout Run, known at the time as Potter's Flats, as this was the same property conveyed to Leonard Morey by General James Potter's estate. Here Reuben, described as a man of great energy, laid out the property in building lots to establish a village that would become Benezette.

ELK COUNTY -THE BEGINNING

On April 18, 1843, the Commonwealth of Pennsylvania passed an act establishing five counties including Elk County. Elk County was formed from parts of Jefferson, Clearfield and Mc Kean Counties. Prior to this time Benezette was a part of Gibson Township, Clearfield County. The Commonwealth appointed intern commissioners that included Timothy Ives, Jr., James W. Guthrie, and Zechariah H. Eddy with authorization to conduct county business, which included surveying the county boundary lines, to acquire land, and to lay out and convey lots, until such a time when the citizens of this new county would elect their own commissioners.

In October of 1843, Reuben Winslow, John Brooks and Chauncey Brockway became Elk County's first elected Commissioners. They notified the appointed commissioners of their election and requested that they turn over their records on the county to them, as specified in the act establishing Elk County. There was a dispute between the appointed and elected commissioners concerning which group had the authority to select the location of the county seat. Reuben Winslow wanted the county seat located at Benezette, while it appeared that the appointed

JAMES L. GILLIS. Picture courtesy of Elk County Historical Society

ISAAC HORTON
Portrait courtesy of Lynda Pontzer

commissioners wanted the county seat in Ridgway. The elected Commissioners prevailed in a legal resolve to this dispute.

On November 6, the County Commissioners held a meeting at John S. Brockway's house in Jay Township. At this meeting the Commissioners ordered that the court of Elk County be held at Hezekiah Warner's House in Caledonia.

Caledonia was the site of first court of Elk County on December 19, 1843. The site the commissioners originally specified as Hezekiah Warner's house was soon changed to the old Caledonia schoolhouse located on the Milesburg Turnpike. Presiding over this court were Associate Judges James L. Gillis and Isaac Horton.

On June 25, 1844, the county commissioners issued a public notice to the people of the county regarding the matter of locating the county seat:

The citizens of Elk County and the public generally are hereby respectfully notified that the commissioners of said county have no knowledge of any seat of justice being fixed for the county of Elk.

And whereas, it is reported that lots are soon to be exposed for sale in the town of Ridgway, purporting to be the place where the seat of justice of Elk County has been fixed:

We, the Commissioners of said county, inform the public generally, that we do not know that there is any seat of justice fixed for said county at Ridgway, or any other place, consequently we do not recognize the town of Ridgway as the seat of justice, and feeling desirous that the people, before they purchase lots in the town of Ridgway, under the impression that they are purchasing lots in the town where the seat of justice, of Elk County has been fixed, should be apprised of the above facts, we therefore solicit attention to this notice.

On June 26, the meeting was adjourned to reassemble at Brockway's on September 16, but by some arrangement, the commissioners met at David Thayer's house in Ridgway. After that day's business was transacted, they considered the house too small, and held their meetings in Erasmus Morey's home at Ridgway. On September 19, proposals for donations of moneys or lands for the location of the county seat were called for. C. Brockway dissented; but replies were so unsatisfactory, that the time had to be extended.

On July 1, John J. Ridgway and his wife Elizabeth sold (through their legal agent Jonathan Colegrove) for $20, Town Lot No. 116 to Z. Henry Eddy, for the use of Elk County. On December 16, 1844, Ridgway was selected as the county seat for Elk County.

BENEZETTE – THE TOWN – THE TOWNSHIP

In Benezette Township's first election for officers on February 1846, the Winslow family played a key role in the development of the township. E.E. Winslow was elected Justice, Carpenter was elected as one of two supervisors, R.C. Winslow was elected one of six School Board members together with serving as township clerk, and Charles Winslow was elected as one of two fence viewers.

By 1850, Reuben's village of Benezette was a thriving Elk County community. The town population consisted of 243 citizens with thirty-six houses, twenty-seven farms and a number of businesses. R.M. & D. Winslow were town merchants.

Winslow Hill received its name from George Wait Winslow who farmed a 200-acre parcel on the Hill once known as Mt. Pleasant. George was the nephew of Reuben, the son of Carpenter and Elizabeth who lived on the farm with him in their later years.

THOMAS B. WINSLOW – CIVIL WAR OFFICER

It appeared apparent in the early part of 1861, that a major conflict between the northern and southern states was inevitable. Thomas L. Kane, an attorney, was an active abolitionist who lobbied Governor Curtain for authorization to raise a regiment of men from Mc Kean, Elk, and Cameron Counties to meet this threat. It was Kane's belief that Pennsylvania loggers and woodsmen would make excellent soldiers in that they were free spirited men, accustomed to hard work, knew the ways of woods, and were very handy with a rifle, as dinner often depended upon their marksmanship .

Once the governor granted Kane's request, Kane went to work recruiting men. Kane came to Benezette seeking assistance to raise men. He

BUCKTAIL STATUE LOCATED IN DRIFTWOOD, PENNSYLVANIA

met with Cole (probably Caleb) Winslow, a local lumberman, to help in this endeavor. Within twenty-four hours, Winslow, with help from his nephew Thomas B. Winslow and John A. Wolfe, was able to sign up 109 men from the Elk County area for this cause. The group assembled at Benezette and elected Thomas Winslow as Captain and thus formed the Elk County Rifles, Company G. The new, raw, untrained group of recruits then proceeded to Driftwood to meet the other two companies Kane recruited. This group called themselves the Bucktails. A monument depicting the Bucktails and commemorating their courage stands in a special square in Driftwood.

Kane's Bucktails built rafts and floated down river to Harrisburg. At Harrisburg, Winslow, due to the small number of men comprising the Elk County Rifles, worked out an arrangement with Hugh Mc Donald, a captain of a group of about the same size from Tioga County, to merge the two units. Winslow, being aware that Mc Donald was a veteran of the Mexican War with knowledge in military matters, felt it was in the best interest of the unit to withdraw his name from election in favor of Mc Donald. During the beginning of the Civil War, captains were selected by a vote of the men in the unit.

Thomas B. Winslow was promoted on January 11, to first lieutenant. He was wounded in the fighting near Harrisonburg, Virginia, when a shell fragment hit him. He was captured at Catlett's Station, Virginia, on August 22, 1862, and confined in Richmond. He was released on September 24, 1862, and sent to Camp Parole, Maryland. Winslow rejoined the regiment in time to participate in the Battle of Fredericksburg on December 13, 1862, where he was again wounded, this time a flesh wound, the bullet having passed through his left hip. He was in command of Company K during the battle, a post he held from October 31, 1862, until February 28, 1863. He was out of action for over a month as it was noted that his wound had not healed by January 15, 1863. In mid June 1863, Winslow was detached from the regiment to perform recruiting duty at Clearfield. In January to February of 1864, he was on recruiting service in Washington D.C., and again in March and April of the same year at Harrisburg. Winslow mustered out with the regiment on June 11, 1864.

WINSLOWS – THE MAYFLOWER CONNECTION

Kenelm was the first direct ancestor who arrived in North America, of the Winslows who settled Benezette. Although Kenelm played a key role in the early development of the Plymouth Colony, he did not arrive on the Mayflower's first voyage here with his brother Edward. He came several years later in 1629.

Carpenter's son Carpenter, who came to Pennsylvania with his father to settle about 1820, married Beulah Keene whose ancestry can be traced back to John Alden, Priscilla Mullins, William Bradford, William Brewster, and Richard Warren, all distinguished members of the Plymouth Colony. The chart below traces Carpenter and Beulah's ancestry back to these notable forefathers. Read the chart from the top to the bottom.

Carpenter Winslow's wife was
Beulah Keene's the daughter of
Celannah Wadsworth's daughter of

Abigail Bradford' daughter of	Abigail Bradford's mother	Abigail Bradford's father	
Gamaliel Bradford daughter of	Abigail Bartett's mother	Samuel Bradford' father	Abigail Barlett's father
Hannah Rogers daughter of-	Ruth Peabody's mother	William Bradford's father	Benjamin Bartlett's .
Elizabeth Pabodle daughter of			Sarah Brewster's .
Elizabeth Alden' parents	Elizabeth Alden's parents		Love Brewster's father
JOHN ALDEN	**PRISCILLA MULLINS**	**WILLIAM BRADFORD**	**WILLIAM BREWSTER**

Carpentor Winslows's wife
Beulah Keene's father
Willaim Keene's father
Hezekiah Keene's father
Josiah Keene's mother
Abigail Littles's mother
Anna Warren's father's

RICHARD WARREN

Replica of Mayflower moored at Plymouth Harbor.

WINSLOW – SHORT STORIES

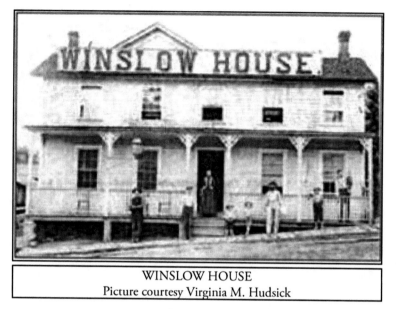

WINSLOW HOUSE
Picture courtesy Virginia M. Hudsick

GEORGE LAFAYETTE WINSLOW was born in Benezette on October 1847 in the woods during the Great Flood of 1847, the son of Ebenezer (Eben) and Elizabeth Hicks Winslow. At the age of fifteen his father died, leaving him to depend upon his own resources. At this young age he became a successful logger, and made enough money to pursue other interests. In 1871, Winslow, rented the Benezette Hotel which he ran for years, after which he operated the Winslow House, a popular hotel in Benezette, until 1889. He left the hotel business to open a meat market in Benezette, which proved to be a very successful venture.

WILLIAM KEENE WINSLOW was born on his father, Charles Keene Winslow's, farm in Benezette

WILLIAM KEENE WINSLOW
Picture courtesy of Bob Nay

in 1875. During his youth he helped his father clear and farm this land. Later in life he would purchase the homestead making his home here. William had a serious injury when he accidentally stepped backwards into a hay chute on the barn floor and fell to the basement causing him to be paralyzed. The doctor, feeling that he had fractured his spine, made arrangements to have him taken to the University Hospital in Philadelphia. As this was

DR. HARRY C. WINSLOW
Picture courtesy of
Lake Shore Visitor

a matter of urgency, preparations were quickly made to have Winslow taken to Philadelphia by train. The train was given direct right-of-way and made the run in record time. Winslow was met at Thirty Second and Market Streets by an ambulance, and rushed to the hospital. An operation was immediately performed, but Winslow died. His wife Mary, sick with cancer, died within the year, never knowing the fate of her husband.

DR. HARRY C WINSLOW was born in Benezette, on July 29, 1884, the son of Charles A. and Mary Ann Burke Winslow, the Grandson of Charles Keene and Rebecca Hicks Winslow. Dr. Winslow, as indicated above, is a Mayflower descendent and a veteran of World War 1. He owned the first radio station of Meadville, Pa., and gave the call letter of his station his daughter Mary G. Winslow's initials – WMGW. He was a former Chairman of the Board of the First National Bank of Meadville, and he later taught school for a time. He attended the University

REBECCA HICKS WINSLOW
Picture courtesy of
Virginia M. Hudsick

of Pennsylvania Medical School and became Chief of Staff at Spencer Hospital in Meadville, and was regarded as a top surgeon of the area.

WILLIAM BURKE WINSLOW was born September 1, 1917, at Benezette, Penna., son of William Alonzo and Gladys Burke Winslow. A veteran of World War II, Winslow was Lt. Colonel, U.S. Air Force B17 Pilot, 306 Bomb Group (H) 367 Bomb Squadron – The Clay Pigeons. Several years following Bill Winslow's passing, a diary was found which recorded his activities as a pilot during World War II. The following is a condensed version of his diary:

Thurleigh, Bedfordshire, England was the home of the 306ᵀʰ Bombardment Group from early September 1942, and continued until long after the end of hostilities in Europe as the 306ᵗʰ group was charged with the aerial mapping of Europe and North Africa, constituted as 306ᵗʰ Bombardment Group (Heavy) on 28 January 1942; activated on 1 March 1942; trained for combat with B-17's; moved to England, Aug-Sept. 1942, and assigned to Eighth AF. During combat, Oct 1942-Apr 1945, this unit operated primarily against strategic targets, striking locomotive works at Lille, railroad yards at Rouen,

WILLLIAM B. WINSLON
Picture courtesy of
Winslow Family

submarine pens at Bordeaux, shipbuilding yards at Vegesack, ball-bearing works at Schweinfurt, oil plant at Merseburg, marshalling yards at Stuttgart, a foundry at Hannover, a chemical plant at Ludwigshafen, aircraft factories at Leipzig, and other objectives on the Continent. William took part in the first penetration into Germany by heavy bombers of Eight AF on 27 Jan 1943 by attacking U-boat yards at Wilhelmshaven. The 306th completed an assault against aircraft factories in central Germany on 11 Jan 1944, being awarded a DUC for the mission. He received another DUCU for action during Big Week, the intensive campaign against the German aircraft industry, 2-25 Feb 1944: although hazardous weather forced supporting elements to abandon the mission, the group effectively bombarded an aircraft assembly plant at Bernberg on 22 Feb. They often supported ground forces and attacked interdictory targets in addition to .strategic operations; helped to prepare for the invasion of Normandy by striking airfields and marshalling yards in France, Belgium, and Germany; backed the assault on 6, Jun 1944 by raiding railroad bridges and coastal guns; assisted ground forces during the St Lo breakthrough in July; covered the airborne invasion of Holland in September; helped stop the advance of German armies in the Battle of the Bulge, Dec 1944-Jan1945 by attacking airfields and marshalling yards; bombed enemy positions in support of the airborne assault across the Rhine in March 1945; remained in the theater after V-D Day as part of United States Air Forces in Europe, and engaged in special photographic mapping duty in Western Europe and North Africa. William Burke Winslow's squadron inactivated in Germany on December 25, 1945.

The Winslows depicted in these profiles all have one thing in common — they are Mayflower descendants as were Ulysses S. Grant, Alan B. Sheppard, Jr, and President Franklin D. Roosevelt , to mention just a few. These ancestors came to America seeking freedom and opportunity. They came in a small wooden sailing ship through the cold turbulent December waters of the Atlantic Ocean to the unsettled coast of New England. It was a hazardous trip which took over 60 days. Here in this primitive land they carved out an existence, overcame many severe hardships and tribulations, and built a cornerstone for a new country which offered liberty and freedom for all citizens. These Winslow descendants would go on to make many more contributions to this nation. They did not flinch from the wounds received at the battle of Fredericksburg or the flak from enemy war planes over the skies of Germany. Their dream was to endure. From the establishment of the Plymouth Colony to the founding of Benezette, the Winslow family has a rich and proud heritage in the history of this nation.

THE END

*Editor's note: Winslow flew a total of twenty-seven missions, and was awarded the Distinguished Flying Cross. William Winslow's notable contribution was one of many made by veterans of this bloody war, and in his memory we dedicate the Winslow Story to those veterans.

Research the transition of the intern commission

Individuality, "Seventeenth century"

Eight or ten chests still exist.

Plymouth cupboards are the main contribution of the Colony to American furnishings.

"Metropolitan Museum of Art in New York

Yarmouth was the center of the Winslow families between 1665 & 1673.

History of Jefferson County by Kate M. Scott

Jefferson County History by J.H. Beers

Jefferson County History – Penna - 1982

Renova Daily Record.

History of McKean, Elk, Cameron and Potter Counties by Beers

The Genealogy of William A. Winslow and Gladys M. Burke by Robert Nay

9

THE WEEDS

(Weedville, PA)

Frederick Weed's Gravestone
Picture courtesy of Helen Hughes

The Weed family ancestry in America dates back to June of 1630 when Jonas and John Weed (believed to be Jonas's brother) joined the growing Puritan migration in England and set sail on the flagship *Arabella* for the more tolerant shores of America. The Weed brothers settled just a few miles inland on the Charles River in present day Massachusetts. Jonas and John built their new home on hilly ground just a short distance from the future site of the city Boston. In 1631, this settlement took on the name of Watertown. Jonas, together with other members of the newly formed settlement, signed a document binding them in the support of the Church.

The Liberal Dissident

Jonas, known for his liberal religious views, soon became dissatisfied with the church in Watertown. In 1635, he and John, along with a small group of like-minded settlers, relocated to Connecticut where they founded the town of Wethersfield on the Connecticut River. This was the first white settlement of Connecticut. Thus, Jonas and John are acknowledged as being founding members of both Watertown, Mass., and Wethersfield Conn.

In 1642, Jonas, disagreeing with the more conservative Elder on the administration of the church, relocated from Wethersfield to Stanford, Conn. Again, a small band of like-minded liberal thinking men and their families accompanied him.

Jonas Weed, Jr., was born in Stanford, Conn., in 1647, the sixth child of Jonas Sr. Jonas Jr. was a shoemaker by trade. He was elected Selectman for eleven terms, and participated in Colonial Wars. Jonas Jr. was also a member of the Train Band, which was similar to our present day National Guard, but with much more influence in community affairs.

Sergeant Benjamin Weed

Benjamin Sr. was the second eldest born to Jonas Jr. and Bethia. Benjamin was a Sergeant in Lovewell's expedition against the Indians in Father Rasle's war 1722-26. Sebastian Rasle was a Jesuit Missionary who came to Maine in 1689. He took charge of the Mission to the Abnakis in 1689. There was much turmoil between the Indians, stirred up by these Frenchmen, and the English settlers relative to disputes over the territory. As a result, the Indians began raiding and killing frontier settlers. The French were known to instigate the Indians against the settlers. Due to Rasle's influence with the Indians, the English put a price on his head. The English raided Rasle's camp in 1721, but he managed to escape. In 1724 Sergeant Weed, accompanied a group known as the Lovewell Expedition to raid the Rasle camp. Prior to this raid the Indians killed Lovewell's wife and children when the Indians attacked their settlement. Lovewell and Father Rasle were killed in this raid, but Sergeant Weed miraculously managed to escape.

Benjamin Jr. was born December 16, 1707, the third child of Sergeant Benjamin and Mary. He was a member of the Committee of Safety in Stanford and is listed in the DAR Patriot Index. He died May 28, 1886, at the age of eighty years old and is buried in the North Stanford cemetery. Benjamin was the father of Peter, Fredrick's father.

Peter was born on January 22, 1738, in Stanford, Connecticut. He married Abigail Husted in 1787. Sometime prior to 1791, Peter and Abigail relocated from Stanford to Greenfield, located adjacent to Saratoga Springs, New York. Here they had five children, Frederick being the second oldest, born April 1, 1765.

Frederic Weed - Revolutionary War

At the age of fourteen, Frederick Weed enlisted in the Connecticut Coast Guard under Captain Charles Smith on March 1, 1779, to serve in the Revolutionary War. Frederick later served in the Militia under Captain Reuben Schofield and Isaac Jones. He participated in the battle when the British landed at Stamford, and later in several engagements in New York, near White Plains and Bull Run. Discharged on April 23, 1783, Fredrick's record indicates that he was wounded in the Revolution.

Frederick was a member of **Washington Benevolent Society of Saratoga**, instituted on 22nd day of January 1811.

On September 18, 1787, he married Nancy Hoyt, the daughter of Samuel Hoyt and Dinah Hanford. Nancy was born 16 December 1767, and died 7 August 1855, being 88 years old at the time of her passing. Fredrick and Nancy had four children, all born in Greenfield, New York.

NANCY was born April 1792. She married J. G. Satterless. She died on

December 1, 1856, and is buried at Lock Haven.

ANN M. was born July 1797, and on May 7, 1825, married William F. Luce. Luce came to Jay Township on February 13, 1813, with the Morey and Dwight Caldwell families, together with Ichabod and Sylvester Powers and Captain Joseph Potter. More information on their trip here can be found in the Morey Family History. Luce settled on Gray Hill Road, (the Grays were the last residents to live on the Luce farm), and here he engaged in lumbering and farming. He also had an interest in a sawmill. William and Ann's daughter, Elizabeth Sophia married George Lyman Thurston.

Ann's husband William Luce died on August 14, 1834, at the early age of 38. Ann married for the second time to Potter Goff on August 14, 1836. Potter Golf came to Jay Township to settle in 1817 with his wife and six children and accompanied by his son-in-law Joel Woodworth. His wife died in 1834. He and Ann had one child, Algernon E., who married Caroline Pearsall. Potter died on November 12, 1846, and is buried in a family cemetery plot on Gray Hill Road. Ann died October 8, 1874 and is buried in the Mt. Zion Cemetery

MARY E. was born December 6, 1799. She married Erasmus Morey and they reared a family of four children: Alvina, Lydia (wife of Thomas Tozier of Caledonia), Amelia A., and B.E. Morey. Mrs. Mary Morey   died August 19, 1873. More information on Mary can be found in the Morey family history.

ABIJAH BARABUS and his wife Charolotte came here to settle about 1818.

More on Abijah Barabus just a bit later..

1817 The Move to Bennett's Valley

Frederick Weed's family settled at the mouth of Kersey Run on the Bennett's Branch in 1817, after purchasing a vast tract of land from John Boyd. This land encompassed the area of present day Caledonia and Weedville. Boyd came here about 1814 and located at the mouth of Kersey Run. Here he built the first sawmill on the Bennett's Branch. In 1817, Frederick Weed and Captain Josiah Mead, of Greenfield, who was the father of Judge

Charles Mead of Ridgway, acquired this property. Frederick Weed took possession of the western portion of the Boyd tract which included the sawmill.

Frederick continued operating the sawmill which Boyd had built and made many improvements to the original mill. Frederic was also a tanner, harness maker, and currier, dressing and finishing leather by trade. About 1820 he built the first tannery on the Bennett's Branch, together with a grist mill at his settlement which would become known as Weedville.

Fredrick died September 18, 1845, at the age of eighty, He is the only Revolutionary War Veteran buried in the Weedville Cemetery. Residing next to him is his wife Nancy Hoyt Weed who died on September 17, 1856.

The Weed tradition lived on, as Frederick willed all his property and money to his only son Abijah. Abijah Barnabas Weed was born January 14, 1790. On December 4, 1817, he married Charlotte Mead at Greenfield, and came to Elk County, Pennsylvania in 1818. Charlotte was born January 3, 1796. Three "Meads" are recorded in the Colonial Dames book. Abijah was elected Judge in Jay Township's first election for officers held on February 27, 1844. Later he served as Inspector of Elections and Overseer of the Poor for Jay Township. Abijah died January 27, 1862. Abijah and Charlotte's children included :

> PETER FREDRICK was born in Saratoga County in 1818. In 1843 he married Thelma Andrews from Clearfield County.
> BARNEY ABIJAH was born December 26, 1820. Barney was Jay Township's first elected Justice. He married Mary Ann Turley on January 2, 1853. Mary Ann was born September 1832, died December 13, 1917.
> MANLY
> NANCY M. MEAD
> ANELTHY M. TURLEY(?)
> JUSTUS P. was born December 18, 1831. Justus worked for his father until 1854 when he was twenty-three years of age and he married E. J. Tudor, daughter of John and Elizabeth (Hunter) Tudor who came to Weedville in 1853. Mr. and Mrs. Weed had three children: Abijah B., Manley E. and Eva E. (wife of J.H.

Webb, Falls Creek, Penna).

J.H. Webb was born in Weedville, the son of William M and F. Elizabeth (Morey) Webb. Mr. Weed purchased a farm in Jay Township, and in 1882 engaged in the mercantile business in Weedville. Justus played an active role in the welfare and growth of the community and held various Jay Township offices.

Justus has the distinguished honor of being Weedville's first Postmaster.

The Weed family had a glorious history as pioneer settlers in the growth of our county: from Watertown, Mass. in 1630; from Wethersfield, Connecticut's first white settlement; from Stanford, New York where Frederick had a distinguished service record in the Revolutionary War; to a settlement at the mouth of Kersey Run on the Bennett's Branch, the present day town of Weedville.

THE END

History of McKean, Elk, Cameron and Potter Counties by Beers
History of Pennsylvania by Egle
Tozier and Allied Families by Gladys A. Tozier
"Looking For Ephraim" by Helen Hughes

The Webbs

From the 14th to the 21st. Century

Webb Town, USA

The village of Force, once known as Webb Town, was founded by Isaac Webb in the early eighteen hundreds. The roots of the Webb Family tree reach out across the Atlantic Ocean to the days of knights in shining armor dedicated to the services of King Henry VII & VIII, and to the Regent Court of Queen Catherine Parr of England, as well as to the Goble Theater and the family of the famed playwright William Shakespeare. Migrating to America in 1629, the Webbs left

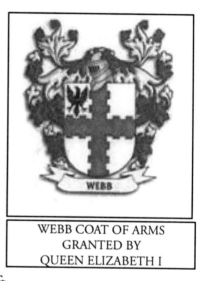

WEBB COAT OF ARMS
GRANTED BY
QUEEN ELIZABETH I

a lasting legacy as distinguished pioneers of New England and as American patriots on various battlefields of the Revolutionary War.

We turn the pages of time back to 1350, to Henry Webb for the purpose of tracing Isaac's ancestors from Warwickshire, England to Force, Pa.

(1) Henry Webb, born May 1350, Warwickshire, England

(2) GEOFFREY WEBB, son of Henry, was born on April 1372, in Stratford.

(3) **JOHN WEBB**, son of Geoffrey, was born on January 5, 1404/5, Stratford.

(4) **WILLIAM WEBB**, son of John was born March 16, 1425, in Stratford. William was Lord Mayor of London during the

reign of Henry VII

(5) **SIR JOHN ALEXANDER WEBB**, son of William was born July 9, 1450, In Oldsrck. Sir John was a Knight in the King's army.

When Henry VIII separated the Church of England from the Catholic Church, first cousins were permitted to marry. This occurred among the Webbs, Ardens and Shakespeares. This may help explain the following interchange of these names.

(6) **SIR JOHN ALEXANDER WEBB, JR.**, (1484-1516) son of John Sr., was born January 11, 1484, Stratford. John was an officer of rank in King Henry's VIII's army. Sir John had four children which included Sir Henry Alexander Webb, Mary, Abigail, and Margaret.

(6A) SIR HENRY JOHN ALEXANDER WEBB. This son of Sir John was born Mary 11, 1510. Sir Henry was an usher in the Privy Council of Catherine Parr, Queen Regent of England, the 6th wife of King Henry VIII. Queen Catherine to extinguish a debt, and for Henry John's services to the Crown, along with his friendship with the Queen, or as the Queen put it, "her trusty and well beloved servant," granted lands and estates in Dorsetshire to Sir Henry which were passed down to his descendants. King Henry VIII later confiscated these same lands during his suppression of the Catholic Church.

On June 17, 1577, Sir Henry was granted by Queen Elizabeth I a Webb Coat of Arms in recognition of personal and meritorious service to the Crown. This established the Webbs as a family of nobility that passed from generation to generation.

The cross on the Webb Coat of Arms indicates that the ancestor was with King Richard Court de Leon in the 3rd Crusade. The dual crown in the crest was given to those who had been in the service of one of the sovereign dukes of The French Confederation, and the eagle shows that the ancestor had won a battle at sea while in command of the vessel in which it was fought.

John Alexander Webb, Jr. had two daughters, Abigail and Mary. Abigail married Richard Shakespeare and they had a son John. Mary married Robert Arden, and they had a daughter Mary. Abigail's son married Mary's daughter, forming a union between first cousins John Shakespeare and Mary Arden.

John Shakespeare and Mary Arden were the parents of the famous English playwright William Shakespeare. How ironic that the parents of the most brilliant bard of all times were illiterate. There is a song called "I'm my own Grand Pa," but in reality, as a result of citizens being allowed to marry their first cousins, sisters Abigail and Mary Webb were both grandmothers of William Shakespeare.

William Shakespeare, as almost everyone knows, was an English poet and playwright, now widely regarded as the greatest writer in the English language and the world's pre-eminent dramatist. His surviving works consist of 38 plays, 154 sonnets, two long narrative poems, and several other poems. His plays have been translated into every major living language and are performed more often than those of any other playwright.

(7) **MARGARET,** Sir Henry John Alexander Webb's daughter, sister to Mary and Abigail, married Alexander Webb, son of Sir Henry Alexander Webb and Grace Arden. Margaret was a direct ancestor of Isaac Webb, the founder of Force. Margaret and Alexander had a son named Sir Alexander Webb,

Estate Sale 1635

(8) **SIR HENRY ALEXANDER WEBB JR.,** (1559 - 1629) and his four sons sold the land and Estates in Dorsetshire which were given to the Webbs by Queen Catherine. These vast real-estate holdings, held for less than 100 years, had become extremely valuable. This landfall sale financed their courageous move to America. Alexander and his four sons set the Webb Family roots in this great new world.

(9) **RICHARD WEBB** (1580 – 1676) was one of the four brothers who accompanied his father to America in 1629, and settled at Norwalk, Connecticut.

To his first wife Grace Wilson, he had four children. When she died he married Elizabeth Gregory. When Richard died in `1676, he willed his entire estate to his second wife Elizabeth Gregory Webb, leaving his sons to fend for themselves.

> **(10) RICHARD WEBB, JR.,** (1611-1675) was the oldest of four boys, born in Norwalk, Dorset England. It would appear that Richard, Jr. accompanied his father in coming to America. Richard, Jr., married Margery Moyer.

Cambridge 1635

In October, 1635, Richard Webb was one of sixteen intrepid pioneers, under the inspiration and direction of Thomas Hooker, who journeyed over one hundred miles with their cows, horses and swine, from Newtown (Cambridge) in the Massachusetts Bay to settle in a place known to the Indians as Suskeaug, meaning "black earth," due to the rich soil of the fertile meadows.

Thomas Hooker, Founder of American Democracy

Thomas Hooker, born in England, was a minster who came to America to escape religious persecution in 1633, and settled at Newtown, now known as Cambridge. In Newtown, Hooker soon became very popular in the settlement for his views that government should be founded on the consent of the governed. However, his views were not shared by the other ministers of the colony who believed that only church members should have the right to vote. Inspired to start a new settlement, and to completely free himself from the leaders of the Massachusetts Colony, Hooker and his followers moved west to establish the first English settlement in Connecticut. Here he implemented the "The Fundamental Orders of Connecticut," the first constitution in the New World which was a set of rules establishing a government of people, by the people, and for the people. Hooker is known by most historians as the Father of American Democracy.

Thomas Hooker's settlement was first named Newtown. Figure 1 shows a plot plan drawn by a surveyor of the times by the name of William S. Porter. Here Richard Webb became one of the sixteen founding members of this settlement and built a typical rustic pioneer hut or "Dug-out," and taking up residence upon a hundred acre parcel located near a road from Little River to North Meadow.

The following illustrations indicate a crude layout of the original village of Newtown. As noted, Richard Webb's lot is shown in the bottom left hand corner of the town square.

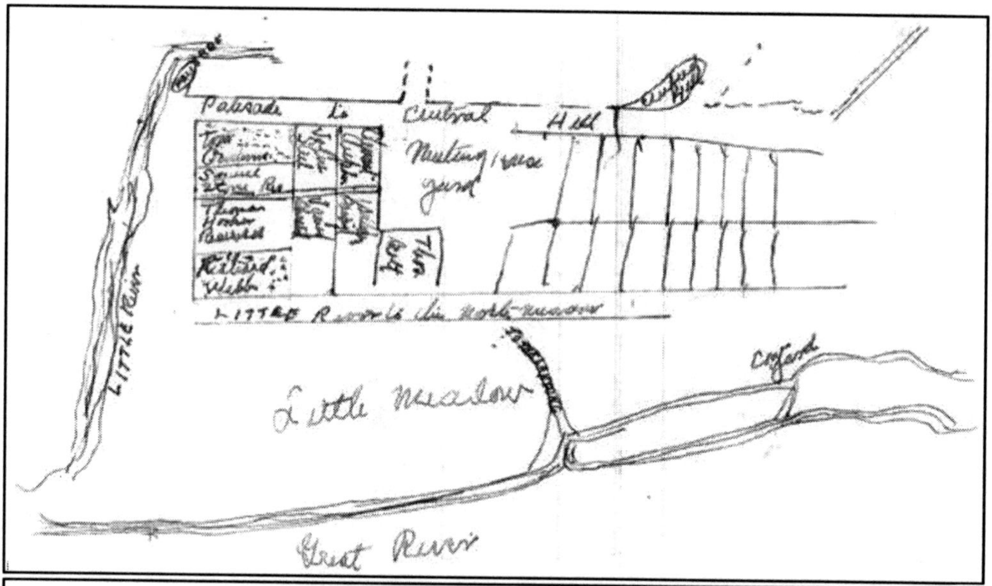

Figure 1 – Showing original layout of Hartford, Connecticut, 1637

Hartford, Connecticut 1637

In 1637, Newtown was renamed Hartford, to honor the English town of Hertford. Hartford served as the capital of Connecticut Colony until 1701, when the New Haven Colony merged with Hartford thus creating two capitals. In 1875 Hartford became the sole capital of Connecticut.

Hartford's Founders Plaque is located on Main Street between the Old City Hall and the Hartford Public Library and lists the sixteen founders including Richard Webb.

Hartford's founder plaque (Shown in figure #2) is inscribed:

In memory of the courageous ADVENTURERS who inspired and directed by Thomas Hooker journeyed through the wilderness from Newtown (Cambridge) in the Massachusetts Bay to Suckiaug (Hardford)-October 1635.

The names of the Hartford founders are indicated below the inscription, which includes the name of Richard Webb. Note the inscription refers to these pioneers as "Adventurers". This is because at the time this settlement was formed, it was a most dangerous and perilous endeavor. They settled near a tribe of Suskeaug Indians and a Dutch settlement which posed a threat to the English. In addition to a land known for extremely harsh winters and cantankerous neighbors, the title to this land was in dispute.

The descendants of Richard Webb, ancestor of Isaac Webb, can legitimately claim eligibility for membership in the Society of Descendants of the Founders of Hartford, Inc.

About 1651, Richard sold his land in Hartford and moved to Stamford where he had acquired land. In Stamford, he was elected Selectman in March 29, 1655. He was the town surveyor 1656, and in 1659 he was voted a seat in the meeting house.

On December 14, 1660, Richard was voted land in Norwalk River, where he died in 1675.

    (11) SAMUEL WEBB (1662-1736) Richard's son, father of Charles. Married Hannah Jagger

    (12) CHARLES WEBB (1697 – 1739) Samuel's Son, father of Charles, Jr. Married Mary Smith.

Continental Army Colonel Charles Webb

Isaac's father, Charles Webb was born February 13, 1724, in Stamford, Fairfield County, Conn., the youngest of six children born to Charles and Mary Smith Webb.

On July 16, 1747, Charles Webb married Mercy Holly (April 12, 1719 – April 1800) in Stamford, Conn. They had six children. Isaac Webb was the youngest.

According to the town records of Stamford, Charles Webb was very active in civic affairs. He was a very prominent and popular leader who was elected selectman, a position he would be re-elected to nineteen times! In 1758, he was elected as a Representative, and re-elected three times. While serving in this position he was opposed to the demands of the Crown. Col. Charles Webb in 1768 was entitled by vote to the 3rd seat in the Meeting House.

In 1760, Charles attained the rank of Captain in the Continental Army. In 1775, he was sent by the Continental Congress on a military mission to investigate the situation at Ticonderoga, to which he made a satisfactory report on June 8th. In July 1775, he was commissioned by the legislature as a colonel and was put in charge of the Seventh regiment of the State Militia stationed at Greenwich. In September, Charles was ordered to New Hampshire, and from his camp on Wintor Hill he wrote that he was prepared for any service to which General Washington might call him. In 1775, Col. Charles Webb's regiment was ordered to Boston Camp to serve under General George Washington. He was discharged on December 10, 1775, and re-enlisted in 1776. It was not uncommon for continental soldiers to resign in the winter and re-enlist in the following spring.

Col. Webb in October 28, 1776 fought with the 19th Continental Army in the battle of White Plains and was officially recognized in this battle as a bold officer. This battle was an inconclusive engagement. General William Howe's British army, with Hessian support, was completing their occupation of New York and surrounding areas. George Washington withdrew to the high ground near the village of White Plains. A certificate dated September 1, 1777, indicates that Washington requested for his regiment the following supplies: 3,234 gallons and 2 pints of beer, 121 pounds of butter, 20 ½ pounds of candles, 183 gallons and 7 pints of meal, and 38 gallons and 3 pints of pease porridge.

In December of 1777, Colonel Charles Webb participated in brisk action at the Battle of White Marsh where his regiment absorbed the attack of the Hessians. This battle was fought in the area surrounding White Marsh, Pennsylvania. The battle, which took the form of a series of skirmish actions, was the last major engagement of 1777 between British and American forces. British commander General William Howe led a sizable contingent of troops out of British occupied Philadelphia in one last attempt to destroy George Washington and the Continental Army before the onset of winter. Washington repelled the British attacks, and Howe returned to Philadelphia without engaging Washington in a decisive conflict. With the British back in Philadelphia, Washington was able to march his troops to winter quarters at Valley Forge.

Colonel Webb resigned his commission on March 13, 1778, due to disability contracted in service. His son Charles, who also fought in the Revolution, was killed on a gun boat in the sound. He had married Elizabeth Smith of Stamford,

Colonel Webb was a member of the Society of the Cincinnati which was founded in May, 1790, at the Verplank house, Fishkill, New York, by Continental Army officers who fought in the American Revolution. Of the 5500 officers in the Revolutionary Army who were eligible to join, about 2,150 did so. George Washington was elected the first President General of the Society in December 1793, and served until his death in 1799. Alexander Hamilton succeeded him.

Isaac Webb- Revolutionary War

Isaac Webb was born July 28, 1766. As a young lad he served as a private in the Revolutionary War, probably in the capacity of a drummer boy, and generally in a unit under the command of his father the Colonel. His military records indicate that Isaac in May of 1775 was a private in Captain Jonathan Dimon's Company from Fairfield. He also served as a private in the 6th Company, Captain Edward Shipman's 7th Regiment, under the command of his father from July 11, 1775 to December 18, 1775, when he was discharged. In April 27, 1777, he re-enlisted for 5 days as a private in Captain Dan Platt's Company in the 7th Regiment, under the command of Lt. Colonel William Worthington who marched in alarm to New Haven. In October 5 to 22, 1777,

Isaac served as a private in Captain Ebenezer Hill's Company in Colonel Samuel Whiting's Regiment at Fishkill.

CHILDRED OF
ISAAC & MARY HUSTED WEED WEBB

Mary Ann Webb – (10 16, 1794 – 10- 31, 1795)
William Morris Webb – (12-19- 1796 – 3- 25-1800)
George Webb – (January – 8, 1800)
Charles Webb – (Approx 1806)
Angelina Webb – (February 6, 1812)

Isaac married Mary, the daughter of Peter & Abigail Husted Weed. Mary (October 1771 – January 1849) was born in Stamford County, Conn. They had five children. The dates would indicate that the Webb and Weed families knew each other before coming here to settle.

CHARLES WEBB

1000 acres: The Founding of Webb Town

Sometime between 1809 and 1818, Isaac Webb purchased 1000 acres of land two miles above the confluence of Kersey Run and the Bennett's Branch He and his family moved from Saratoga, New York, to settle on this land. Ebenezer Hewitt preceded Isaac here by several months and purchased a large track of land just south of Isaac's property. Isaac's son Charles would later marry Caroline, the daughter of Ebenezer and Sarah Hewitt.

Isaac was a surveyor by trade and was described as a man whose memory was prodigious. He was known throughout the area as "The Colonel", which he likely usurped from his father, as he never obtained a rank above a private.

Here, on this newly purchased 1000 acres, Isaac began the development of the village of Webb Town by building and operating a saw mill, gristmill and store. The mills would later pass to his son Charles, and Charles in turn would pass the mills over to his son Zenas M.

Charles kept an Account Ledger, dated 1841 to 1863, of the gristmill's operations, which has survived the generations. The following are several selected entries from this ledger.

1842 - Isaac Coleman Cr.

April 2 - to Five Dollars Cash	5.00
To thirty of flour	.75
To one bushel & half of Corn	1.12 ½

1843 – Thomas Hewitt, Dr.

Novr. 5 - to use of Wagon four Day	.75
May 1844 – to one bushel of oats	.37 ½
	$1.12

1844- Israel Nichols, Dr.

Aug. 10 - to 506 Feed of Boards	1.74
July – to Carrying Wool to Machine	.75

1844 - Schuyler Crandall, Cr.

To 10 ½ Days Work at 40 pr. Day	4.20

1845 - Franklin Hewitt, Dr.

March 6 - to ¼ Day Rafting	.56
" " 7 - to one Day Making Grubs	.62 1/2
	1.18 1/2

1845 - Leonard Morey, Dr.

April 5 - to 824 lbs. of hay at 50	4.12
April 22 - to 500 " of hay " "	2.50

1859 – DANIEL HEWIT, Dr. (rye and flour)

Feb. 17 – one Pair of Shoes	1.75
June - one Pige	1.00

1845 - John Macumber, Sen., Dr.

March - to on ox yoke	1.00
July to Carrying Wool to the mase	.50

1845 - Selah Morey, Dr.

Decm. 26 - To five Du. Of Apples at 25 pr.	1.25

1860 - Star Denison, Cr.

Dec. 22 - To five Dollars in hand.

In 1844, a portion of land, including Jay and Benezette Townships, was carved from Clearfield County to form Elk County. At this time Morris and Charles Webb were listed as owners of a saw & gristmill and resident taxpayers of Huston Township, or rather that part of the township belonging to Elk County. Jay Township was once part of Huston Township, Clearfield County. In Jay Township's first election in Elk County, William Webb was elected first Township Treasurer.

Raymond Nelson tells a story about Grandma Webb. We assume Grandma Webb would have been either Emily or Harriet. As the story goes, one calm, quiet, still day in July, the sort of a day that in your bones you knew a storm was imminent, Grandma related that she could hear the distant rumbling of what sounded like thunder. Later, she learned that what she actually heard was the cannon fire from the Battle of Gettysburg. Isaac Wheeler told a similar story, claiming that while hunting near Buckpoint in the Trout Run Area, he heard the cannonading from this same battle. A few months later Isaac enlisted in the Union Army.

Lemonade Lucy

A granddaughter of Isaac Webb wrote to her cousin in Iowa – "Oh, why did our fathers have to bring us out into this God -forsaken Country, when we might have stayed where there was a chance to do as our cousin Lucy Webb and marry a President".

This reference is to First Lady Lucy Ware Webb Hayes, wife of President Rutherford B. Hayes, or Lemonade Lucy, as many affectionately knew her for her refusal to serve alcoholic beverages in the White House.

Alexander Webb was a common ancestor to both Lucy Ware Webb Hayes and Isaac Webb. When Alexander came to America in 1629 with his four sons, one son, William, was an ancestor of First Lady Lucy Hayes; another son, Richard, was Isaac's GGG Grandfather.

Webb Town becomes Force

As three generations passed, the Webb name began to disappear from the census roles in Webb Town. Isaac's granddaughter, Erminia, the daughter of Charles and Caroline Hewitt Webb, married Jack Force in 1860. The citizens of the area began calling the town Force.

Private Isaac Webb, a Revolutionary War Veteran, is buried in a family Cemetery plot on the south side of a town named after him, Webb Town (Force).

Conclusion

It would be challenging for even a brilliant playwright like William Shakespeare to compose an imaginary drama to rival the true life history of the Webb family. But, suppose that William Shakespeare could be resurrected for the purpose of writing a play to present a true portrayal of the Webb Family history. Would the fact that he has Webb's blood flowing in his veins cause him to unduly enhance his relatives? Perhaps not, but how would he describe the grandeur of the Webb Knights who served under Kings Henry VII and VIII? Or, how would this brilliant playwright handle the encounters of Sir Henry John Alexander Webb as usher in the Privy Council of Queen Catherine Parr, or his feelings when granted a Webb Coat of Arms by Queen Elizabeth I? How would he dramatize, on his stage, the Webb family history; the rationality of Alexander Webb, a prominent and wealthy citizen of England, who sold off his extensive land holdings to migrate to America, a far away primitive land? Or, how would he present Richard's adventuresome deeds as one of the founders of a settlement in the primitive and perilous land of Connecticut, a settlement that later would become Hartford? Or, how would the play depict Colonel Charles Webb charging his rag -tag band of Continentals against the world's strongest army; or the fortitude of Charles's son Isaac in establishing a village in the wilds of Pennsylvania. Questions, questions, and more questions, all ask for hypothetical answers. Surely a Hollywood producer, knowing this story, could not resist the temptation of making these notable plots into an award winning production. Beginning with the first known Webb ancestor who accompanied King Richard on the Crusades, to Isaac Webb, who established a lasting village in the Allegany Mountains on the Bennett's Branch, a producer would have a wealth of color in which to weave a great drama.

THE END

WIKIPEDIA – FREE ENCYCLOPEDIA
CENSUS RECORDS 1850 TO 1920
OLD FAMILY GENEALOGY – AUTHOR UNKNOWN
LYNN S. NICKLAS – DAR
STATE OF CONNECTICUT, MILITARY DEPARTMENT, ADJUTANT GENERAL'S OFFICE
ACCOUNT LEDGER – RAYMOND NELSON
HISTORY AND GENEALOGY OF THE GOV JOHN WEBSTER FAMILY OF CONN.
BY WILLIAM HOLCOMB WEBSTER & REV. MELVILLE REUBEN WEBSITE

NOAH KINCAID AND FAMILY

A Forgotten Gravestone

A number of years ago while hunting small game in a thick patch of laurel, I discovered a forlorn gravestone. Needless to say I was quite surprised to find a tombstone here in the midst of this

LYDIA HOUGH KINCAID'S
Gravesite on Rock Hill
Picture by James Burke

brush and debris, but when I read the inscription on the stone I was flabbergasted - "Lydia Hough Kincaid, who departed this Life, February – 1841, Age 62 years, 3 months, 29 days." "WOW!" I thought, this grave is old; she died before the Civil War.

Little did I know at the time, nor would I find out until many years later, that the woman buried here, Lydia Hough Kincaid, was wife of the first medical doctor to practice his profession in the county. The mother of the world famous Baptist Missionary, Eugenio, known as the "Hero Missionary" who was an ambassador of goodwill for a President of the United States, and a mother of another son who was the first Sheriff of Elk County, grandmother of Eugenio Hough, a founding father of Los Angles.

The Doctor

DR. NOAH KINCAID
July 15, 1774 - July 22, 1858

Dr. Noah Kincaid, a veteran of the War of 1812, was born in Scotland about 1774, and early in life migrated to Canada. Here he married Lydia Hough. Sometime about 1810 they moved to Potsdam, New York. The family consisted of four sons and three daughters who included Eugenio, born in Wethersfield, Connecticut in 1797, and Eusebuis born in Canada in 1808.

In the early 1820's, the Kincaid family journeyed from New York to homestead on Rock Hill in what is now Jay Township, Elk County. Here Dr. Noah practiced medicine up and down the Bennett's Branch. The evidence strongly suggest that Dr. Kincaid was the first medical doctor to practice his profession in Elk County. Both Dr. Dan Rogers and Jonathan Nichols settled in the Elk County area prior to Noah's arrival here; however, it appears that both of these individuals were more interested and involved in religion rather than medicine. Dr. Dan Rogers came here as a land agent for the New Holland land Co. about 1811, and later moved to Jersey Shore. Jonathan Nichols, and his son-in-law Hezehiah Warner came up the Bennett's Branch with their families in March of 1818, and settled on General Boyd's lands north of Kersey. Jonathan Nichols was a Baptist minster who practiced medicine and farmed.

There was an incident involving Dr. Kincaid and Elder Jonathan Nichols concerning the care for Eliza Gelott. Eliza's brother Erasmus explains this confrontation in a letter to Patent. The following is a copy of his letter.

Dear Patent,

This evening I take the liberty of writing to you again. There has not anything of importance happening since I last wrote to you excepting your son Leonard broke one of the bones in his leg between the knee and ankle. The particulars of it getting broke—he went sleigh riding with the young people up to Doct Kincaids and the sleigh ran against a stumpt and some of them fell on to him and broke it.

Eliza is getting better but I do not think her complaint is removed. Elder Nichols has got home from York State and he has been to see her this evening whether they will have him to doctor her or not, I do not know. They expect that Doct. Kincaid will not consent to it. The Elder says he has had six patients of the kind this last summer.

I began this letter last evening. Elder Nichols and wife staid at my house last nigh. The Elder and Doct Kincaid met at my house today and it was not so pleasant a meeting as I have seen. It was the wish of Richard and Eliza for them, to council together on the subject of Eliza's complaint but Kincaid would not and there was some words that Kincaid had said about the Elder being a Quack—that did not suit the Elder so well but, I believe he is going to take charge of Eliza for a spell.

I remain yours in the bonds of affection,

Erasmus

It would appear from this letter that Dr. Kincaid did not have much confidence in Elder Nichols' qualification as a medical doctor.

The Medicine Cow

The following was published in <u>Brook's Centennial</u> and later republished in <u>"The History of Elk County</u>:

The physician who practiced within the limits of Cameron County was Dr. Kincaid. He settled near the present village of Sterling Run and for years treated the various diseases that flesh is heir to. One incident occurred in his practice that is remembered distinctly by the people who were living in the country at that time, which is somewhat amusing. He was treating a patient at the old Dent place on Bennett's Branch, leaving his saddle bags outside, near the creek. While he went within the house, a certain cow, not having the fear of god Escuaplus before her eyes and instigated by the very spirit of mischief and with malice aforethought proceeded to eat the saddle bags and their contents. When the doctor returned she was quietly chewing the cud. If the proof of the pudding is in the chewing of the bag, by a parity of reasoning that cow should have obtained the full benefit of the medicine, but what was the actual effect upon the animal or what become of her, or how the Doctor replenished his stores, the deponents sayeth not, as history is entirely silent upon those points. We have to add that the doctor was the father of the great Baptist missionary to India, Eugenio Kincaid.

EUGENIO THE MISSIONARY

Eugenio Kincaid, the eldest son of Noah and Lydia, became interested and involved in the Baptist faith at a very young age although his parents were Presbyterian. He was baptized in the DeKalb Baptist Church in New York and later was accepted as a student at the Hamilton Literary and Theological Institution. Eugenio was among five students in the first graduating class of Hamilton in 1822. Hamilton would later become Madison and still later Colgate University. Following his graduation, he assumed the pastorate of the Baptist parish in Galway, New York.

EUGENIO KINCAID
THE HERO MISSIONARY
PICTURE COURTESY OF BUCKNELL
UNIVERSITY

In 1826, Eugenio moved to Milton, Pennsylvania, and founded the First Baptist Church. Here while he was busy with his duties as a minster, he also was the editor of the Literary and Evangelical Register which was published in Milton. He married a Miss Almy, born at Mount Zion, in 1805. They had two sons, Eugenio Wade Kincaid, born in June, 1827, and Judson Kincaid, born June, 1829.

BURMA

Eugenio became interested in foreign missionary work, and was appointed, along with Reverend Francis Mason by the Executive Committee of the Baptist Union as a missionary to Burma to continue the pioneering work of Dr. Adoniram Judson who had been stationed at Rangoon since July 14, 1813. Within a month before departing for Burma, Eugenio and Almy's infant son Judson died. The Kincaid family departed from Boston Harbor by sail on May 24, 1830, arriving in Burma on November 27th the following year. About a year after arriving in Burma, the Kincaids had a third son who also died, and tragedy once again followed when on December 19, 1831, Eugenio's wife Almy died. Despite all these family setbacks and tragedies, Eugenio managed to overcome these crises and began to build a new life in Burma.

The first few years in Burma were a very difficult time for Eugenio. Besides problems with the language barrier, the local government was unreceptive to his struggling efforts. Eugenio was determined to expand the efforts of his predecessor, Dr.

Adoniram Judson, and decided that he would travel into the interior of Burma.

He traveled into areas of Burma that had been previously unknown to the Western World, visiting over three hundred towns and villages. He became quite well known throughout Burma for his many courageous feats which included surveying parts of the country. He learned the various dialects which gave him the opportunity to preach the Baptist word of Christianity to the native tribes of the country in their language. Eugenio, over this period of time, because of his efforts and popularity became known as the "hero missionary."

By 1832, Eugenio was back in Rangoon, and here he met and married Barbara Mc Bain. Barbara was an English woman who was born in Madras Presidency, South India whose father was employed with the East Indian Company. Eugenio and Barbara had two daughters, but tragedy struck once again when his son Eugenio Wade died. In 1842, Eugenio, plagued with persistent health problems, returned home to United States to recover.

Bucknell University

Back home in Pennsylvania, while on leave from Burma, Eugenio worked strenuously in an endeavor to establish a university in Lewistown. Through his ties with the Northumberland Baptist Association, the organization initiated the planning and fund-raising for the new university. In 1845, Eugenio working with Reverend Joel E. Bradley convinced Professor Stephen Taylor, who had recently resigned from the faculty of Madison University, to join the new venture in Lewisburg. Taylor was an experienced educator with practical expertise and skills in the organizational and curricular structuring of an academic institution. Eugenio canvassed extensively throughout Pennsylvania and New Jersey between 1847 and the closing of the subscription period on January 9, 1849. His dedication to cause and tireless efforts in this project were instrumental in the founding of Lewistown

University. He served on the Board of Trustees of Lewistown University from 1846 to 1850. In 1886, Lewistown University would become known as Bucknell University.

Ambassador of Goodwill

In 1850, his work done in Pennsylvania, Eugenio returned to Burma, and his first order of business was to meet with the new King of Burma who was interested in developing trade with United States. The King invited Eugenio to visit the Royal Court and allowed him to preach under government sanctions. Eugenio Kincaid's command of the Burmese language and knowledge of their customs enabled him to serve as an ambassador of goodwill between the two countries. In 1857, he traveled back to the United States as an official messenger and translator for the King of Burma and President James Buchanan. Before returning to Burma in 1858, Eugenio Kincaid was awarded an honorary Doctorate of Divinity by the Lewistown University.

Kincaid retired from missionary work in 1865 and settled in Giard, Kansas until his death on April 3, 1883. His second wife died soon after, on April 27. Eugenio Kincaid certainly had a remarkable career both as a missionary and educator. His dedication to principle and strength of character became symbols of Bucknell University. Eugenio encouraged the university's first international student, Burmese native Mauna Shaw Loo, Class of 1864, to come to Lewisburg.

EUSEBUIS – ELK COUNTY'S FIRST SHERIFF

Eusebuis, Noah and Lydia's second oldest son, was born 1808. He married Samantha Pasco in Elk County. Samantha was born in New Jersey in June 1808, the daughter of Zophar D. Pasco, a member of an old Eastern family who was an early resident of Jay Township. Zophar lived with the Kincaids for several years. Eusebuis and Samantha's family consisted of eight children.

Eusebius was elected the first sheriff when Elk County held its first election for officers on October 10, 1843. He ran on the Democratic ticket and received a total 91 votes. Elk County was formed in 1844, from parts of Mc Kean, Jefferson, and Clearfield Counties. Noah, Eusebius, and Almerin were listed among Jay Township's first resident tax payers in 1844. Both Eusebius and Almerin held various Jay Township offices.

Eusebius, along with Vine S. Brockway and Joseph Rogers, was appointed Court Constable in Elk County's first session of court held in Caledonia on December 19, 1843. Presiding Associated Judges were James I. Gillis and Isaac Horton, both with a proud record in the early history of Elk County. The site of this historic event took place in the school house building once known as the Old Seminary. This building was located along the Milesburg Turnpike, across the road and just a short distance above the future site of Reuben Ingram's general store. This store was first occupied by Loeb's Lumber Company as a company store. Loeb ran a sawmill near the mouth of Laurel Run on the Bennett's Branch.

EUGENIO HOUGH KINCAID –

EUGENIO HOUGH KINCAID

Eugenio Hough Kincaid was the grandson of Noah and Lydia, the second eldest son of Eusebius and Samantha Kincaid. He was born on Rock Hill on March 2, 1833, and received his education in Caledonia. It is not certain where in Caledonia Eugenio Hough was educated. At this time in history, those people living in the Gray Hill and Mt.

Zion area were considered residents of Caledonia. The first school in Jay Township was started in 1822 by Captian Potter Goff on Mt. Zion Road, then known as the Ridge Road. This is probably were Eugenio Hough attended school. It is not known when the Gray Hill School was started.

GRAY HILL SCHOOL HOUSE
Picture Courtesy of Roy Beck

However, the site of this old school house was located within a short distance of the Kincaid residence, and it is remotely possible that he attended school at the Gray Hill School.

In 1850, Eugenio Hough at the age of seventeen accompanied his parents to Wisconsin. By modern day standards this was quite a trip. The family traveled by horse and team to Buffalo, then by boat on the lakes to Detroit. From there they took the Michigan Central Railroad to New Buffalo, and then on to Chicago by boat. In Chicago they took up passage on a Steamer to Milwaukee where they hired a wagon and traveled on to their final destination to lands they purchased in Partage, Wisconsin. Here the family cleared the land and made their new home.

CALIFORNIA GOLD RUSH

Eugenio Hough attended the University of Wisconsin, and later attended a Business College in Madison. He taught school for a short time until news of the gold rush in California gave him itchy feet. In 1857, he was off to California. He sailed into San Francisco during the Golden Age, and from there headed on to Calaveras County where he spent two years mining for gold.

After securing a reasonable profit for his venture, Eugenio retuned home to Wisconsin.

EUGENIO ON THE MOVE

Eugenio spent some time traveling through the States of Mississippi, Texas, Louisiana and Arkansas. He again returned home to Wisconsin, and in the spring of the following year, he traveled by horse and wagon across the central plains to Salt Lake City, Utah. Here Eugenio was employed in building the first telegraph line from Salt Lake City to Ruby Valley, California. Upon completion of the telegraph line he moved on to Sacramento and ran the telegraph company for eighteen months, before deciding to move on to Nevada. The telegraph company later became known as Western Union.

In Nevada, Eugenio ran freight by wagon between Virginia City and Austin, while engaging in some mining. Later he purchased a ranch and raised cattle. The cattle business proved to be a very successful enterprise, and he remained there until 1872, when he decided to sell his ranch and move to Los Angeles.

LOS ANGELES

In California Eugenio purchased fifteen acres of land, and developed one of the finest orange ranches in the area. After raising oranges for a number of years, Eugenio and Mr. Alderson decided to convert the ranch into a business center. This was a very risky venture and many local citizens ridiculed their efforts as a foolhardy endeavor as the Kincaid Ranch was too far removed from the center of population. Eugenio laid out his farm into business lots in 1887. The old Kincaid Orange Grove of yesteryear is today downtown Los Angeles. Kincaid's Orchard was located on what is now the corner of Pico and Figueroa Streets.

Eugenio Kincaid, born and raised in Jay Township, is noted as a true and noteworthy pioneer of the Old West, as his grandparents before him, Noah and Lydia Kincaid were distinguished pioneer settlers of Bennett's Branch.

Some time between 1844 and 1850, Noah, now in his seventies, moved to Sterling Run to live which his daughter Harriett's family. Noah died at the age of 86 and is buried in a small private family cemetery next to his daughter Harriett and her husband Chatham Devling. Carved upon Noah Kincaid's headstone are the dates July 15, 1774 - July 22, 1858. Many of our ancestors would covet, but few of them could claim a legacy as rich as that of the Kincaid family.

THE END

History of McKean, Elk, Cameron and Potter Counties by J.H. Beers
A History of California by J. M. Guinn A.M.
Bucknell University Archives
Looking for Ephraim – Helen Hughes
History of Elk County
Brook's Centennial
History of Jay and Benezette Townships in Bennett's Valley
Eugenio Picture – courtesy of Bucknell University.

Editor's note: Lydia Hough Kincaid's gravesite is located approximately one and one-half miles from the intersection of Mt. Zion Road and Gray Hill Road, located on the left hand side of Rock Hill Road. Efforts are currently underway to make this a historical site.

Artifacts of medical instruments and tools that Dr. Noah Kincaid used during his years as a country doctor are on display at the Cameron County Museum in Sterling Run, Pennsylvania.

JOHNSON FAMILY HISTORY

An 8 foot high granite obelisk in the Grant Cemetery dominates the landscape in this small pioneer graveyard. Veteran flags dance in the tall grass amongst the headstones. Ralph Johnson, one of the earliest settlers on the Second Fork, a Fork known today as the Bennett's Branch, is buried here next to his three wives: Rebecca, Margaret, and Hannah, along with a number of their descendents. As a young adventurous couple, Ralph and Rebecca

RALPH JOHNSON FAMILY CEMETERY PLOT GRANT, PENNSYLVANIA

came to settle here nearly two hundred years ago in 1812. The Grant Cemetery is located a very short distance from the Grant Bridge on the far side of the bank of the Bennett's Branch off of Route 555.

Thew Bethal Johnson, Ralph's father, is buried just a few miles upstream in the Summerson Cemetery near the mouth of Johnson Run. Thew settled here in 1817.

Family cemeteries were a common sight on the early and isolated homesteads of Bennett's Valley. Many of these old family plots are located in hard to find and obscure places owing to changes in the development of the area. Consequently, many of these family cemeteries have been badly neglected over the years.

Some have even vanished from the scene. The family plots of the Kincaid, Morey, Denison, and Lewis families are prime examples of this. The names of the ancestors are literally gone and nearly forgotten.

However, the Johnson family cemeteries are an exception as both the Grant and Summerson Cemeteries appear to have been adequately maintained over the years. A curious person with an interest in life in the early years of Bennett's Valley will study and explore the old tombstones, reading the names, dates, ages, etc. Many questions from the past begin to arise. Who were these people? Where did they come from? How did they get here? What was life like when the settlers first arrived?

Much of the history of the pioneer families of the Bennett's Branch, like the smoke and crackle from yesterday's campfire, has dissipated into the atmosphere, never again to be visualized or heard. Fortunately, enough information on the Johnson family remains; bits and pieces have been gathered from here and there to unfold the history of the family.

Yorkshire, England

Thew Bethuell Johnson was born June 15, 1765, in Walton Parish, Yorkshire, England, the son of Ralph and Ann Fallondonn Johnson. Thew was named after his grandmother Elizabeth Thew. He married Ann, the daughter of Marmaduke and Elizabeth Botterel Simpson on May 18, 1786. Thew was a caretaker of a large estate in Walton Parish where he begat a family of eight children. In 1801, Thew and his family, except for his daughter Lois who remained in England and married James Grugan, decided to migrate to America. The family, a party of nine, included Thew's wife Ann, their sons Ralph, Marmaduke, Thew Jr., John and daughters Betty, Ameline (Ann), and Ellen, booked passage on the Ship *Mary* and set sail from the Port of Hull, England, to the New World. The Johnsons were on the water for an arduous 63 days and arrived in Port of Philadelphia on September 23, 1801.

The following Johnson family members were on board the ship Mary in 1801.

Thew and Ann Johnson,   parents

Ralph Johnson	March 18, 1787
Betty Johnson	October 27, 1788
Marmaduke Johnson	February 29, 1792
Thew Johnson	March 22, 1795
John Johnson	February 21, 1797
Ameline (Ann) Johnson	September 10, 1798, m. Thomas Overturf
Ellen Johnson	born about 1800, m. William Holden

Ships sailing from England to the New World in this period were generally small and over booked, causing very crowded and cramped conditions. Quite often there wasn't sufficient food or water, and as a result a number of passengers died on these trips from various diseases. There isn't any record of the Johnson family voyage; however, owing to the duration of the trip, a logical assumption would be that the family endured many hardships getting to this land called America.

Pennsylvanian Quaker

The Johnson family was Quaker and they were well aware that Pennsylvania was a religious tolerant colony founded by the Quaker William Penn. The Johnsons, like many immigrants before and after them, sought religious freedom along with the economic opportunities in this new land.

In 1805, the Johnsons resided as tenants on the Price Lands in Renovo, Pa. Their eldest son Ralph married Rebecca, the daughter of Benjamin and Elizabeth H. Brooks, and moved up the head waters of the Susquehanna River to settle at Grant (Dry Saw Mill) which was at that time part of Clearfield County, Pike Township. In 1817 this same area would become Covington Township, and later that same year it became Gibson Township.

Still later in the early 1840's this area became part of Elk County, Benezette Township, as the wilderness of the Bennett's Branch began to be tamed.

Son Ralph Comes to Bennett's Branch 1812

Ralph (Thew's son) and Rebecca Johnson came to the Bennett's Branch about 1812, to carve out a home in the wilderness and become the first permanent settlers in what would later be the village of Grant. Five years later in 1817, Ralph's father Thew, together with other members of the Johnson family, would settle upstream on the Branch from Ralph's, at Summerson.

Thew Sr. follows Ralph 1817

In 1817 Thew built two river canoes and followed Ralph's trail up the river. The family traveled in the first canoe, trailing the second canoe filled with what supplies and provisions they would be able to haul, and settled just a few miles up the Bennett's Branch from where Ralph lived. When they reached the spot where they intended to settle, the prime flat land where the village of Grant is now located, they found that a storm had caused a severe blow down of trees on this area. They chose not to clear and clean up the tangled mess. This area would for sometime afterwards be known by the early settlers on the Branch as "The Windfall Bottom". Instead, the Johnsons made a decision to move up the Branch to settle on the other side near the mouth of a small stream, which later would be named Johnson Run. The decision to move up the valley was probably due to the limited planting season and the need to have crops for the following year.

Here they built a small cabin near the bank of the Bennett's Branch, a location known by the Indians and early settlers as Sugar Meadows Bottom, due to a large stand of Sugar Maple trees that grew there. Several of the Johnson descendants claim that the Indians tapped these same trees prior to Thew's arrival. The Johnsons set to work clearing farm land and building and operating a saw mill. Over the years, numerous Indian artifacts were found while tilling the ground.

The foundation stones of Thew's first cabin were still visible until recently. The cabin was located a short distance from where the ford enters the Branch. Thew was apprehensive about what would happen in case the river flooded. One day while Thew was hoeing his corn, as the family story is told, an Indian came traveling by and Thew asked him if he thought his cabin would be safe in the event the Branch flooded. The Indian took Thew's hoe by the handle and held it straight out and said "This High" while nodding his head no. The Indian's advice proved to be accurate as sometime later in 1836 a severe flood washed away the Johnson Cabin, completely destroying all their belongings. The Johnson's were fortunate to escape with their lives, for a number of people perished in this devastating disaster. After the flood, Thew moved to higher ground, just above the first cabin, and built a new home.

Thew died in 1837. The following is his will.

Will of Thew Johnson, Sr., 1765-1837

Gibson Township, Clearfield Co., PA

Dated:	3, March 1836 Probated: 15 June 1837
Wife:	Ann Johnson
Sons:	Thew Johnson, Jr., Ralph J. Johnson, John Johnson, Simpson Johnson, William Johnson
Daughters	Ann, Margaret, Betsy, wife of Jesse Hall Louise, wife of James Grugan, Ellen, wife of William Holden
Granddaughter:	Betsy Johnson, daughter of Ralph J.
Executors:	Simpson Johnson and William Johnson
Witnesses	Thomas Dent and Robert Winn

First, I bequeath unto my beloved wife, Ann Johnson, one comfortable bed and bedding, one beaureau, and some other trifling articles which said Ann may think she wants. My wife to have first choice of beds after my daughters Ann and Margaret have made their choice.

I bequeath unto my daughter Ann one bed and bedding, one cow and two sheep.

I bequeath unto my granddaughter, Betsy Johnson, daughter of Ralph J., one bed and bedding, one cow and two sheep.

Above legacies to be given by my Executors immediately after my decease.

I will that my wife Ann be kept supported and maintained during her natural life at the proper cost and charges of my two sons, Simpson and William., or so long as she shall remain satisfied to live with them, but if she should at any time after my decease think proper to leave the board or residence of said Simpson and William, from that time Simpson and William shall pay or cause to be paid unto here forty dollars per year each and every year during her natural life as dower for her support and maintenance.

I bequeath unto my daughter Ann seventy dollars.

I bequeath unto my daughter Margaret seventy dollars.

I bequeath to my son Ralph J. five dollars.

I bequeath to my son Thew five dollars.

I bequeath to my son John five dollars.

I bequeath to my daughter Betsy, wife of Jesse Hall, five dollars

I bequeath unto my daughter Louisa, wife of James Grugan, five dollars

I bequeath unto my daughter Ellen, wife of William Holden, five dollars.

Said legacies or sums of money to be paid in five years after my decease and not sooner.

I bequeath unto sons Simpson and William all and every part of my real Estate, lands and tenements containing twenty acres, more or less, equally share and share alike.

Lastly, the rest, residue and remainder of my lands and tenements and personal Estate, my half of the Saw Mill and sawed lumber on hand and all my saw longs in the Mill pond or elsewhere together with the remainder of cows, horses, oxen, young cattle, sheep and hogs, and all the grain growing in the ground together with all the hay and grain in the barn binds and cribs of every description, the rest, residue and remainder of beds and bedding, household furniture, kitchen and farming utensils of every description and all the rents and profits and issues arising from my farm now the property of John Pickering as long as the said Pickering may suffer peaceable possession, and all and every remaining part of my personal Estate. I bequeath the same unto my two sons Simpson and William.

Ann, Thew's wife, died two years later on March 8, 1839. Thew and Ann are buried just a short distance from their second home, in a family cemetery plot overlooking the Bennett's Branch in Summerson.

OLD LOGGING CAMP – JOHNSON RUN
Picture courtesy of Glen & Jane Mackey

Thew (1765- 1837) and Ann's Children

According to family history, Thew and Ann had a total or thirteen children but this story can only substantiate 11. Perhaps there was an error in the records or there may have been some infant deaths. The following are the names we know.

1. **RALPH J. JOHNSON** .Born in Yorkshire, England March 10,1787, died-Sept.14, 1857 in Bennett's Valley. He married three times.
   1. Rebecca Brooks (About 1789-Oct 20, 1821)
   2. Margaret Shaffer (About 1792- Step. 14, 1837)
   3. Hannah Jordan (about 1729 - Nov 13, 1865)
2. **ELIZEBETH "BETTEY" JOHNSON** - Born in England October 27, 1788, married Jesse Hall from Humblendon, NY.
3. **LOIS JOHNSON** - (Born June 13, 1791,England. She married James and they had nine children.. Lois did not make the initial journey with her family, but arrived here at a later date.
4. **MARMADUKE JOHNSON** - (Born February 29, 1792)
5. **THEW JOHNSON JR.** – born March 22,1795 in .Yorkshire, England-, died 1867 in Bennett's Valley.
6. **JOHN JOHNSON** - Born February 21, 1797, Walton Parish, Yorkshire. John married Miss Shaffer and they had four children. They lived at Rickeky Station below Renovo, PA.
7. **Ameline (ANN) JOHNSON**- (Sept 10, 1798 England- March 23, 1876) married Thomas Overturf who died April 11, 1864.
8. **ELLEN JOHNSON** - (born 1800 in England -1875) married William Holden.
9. **Margaret Johnson**- born about 1804. Margaret never married and she lived with her brother William in her later years.
10. **Simpson Johnson**- Born about 1804 and died 1860. Simpson was given his mother's maiden name as his first name. He married Therza H. Woodworth(1819-1855).They had five children: Wallace H. , Alziinia A., William Newton, and a boy and a girl who died as infants. Simpson's second marriage was to Azenth (Seeney) Dennison. There were no children to the second marriage.
11. **William Johnson**-Born about 1805, and died Jan 10, 1881. He married Julia Ann Purcell and they had one son

RALPH JOHNSON 1787-1857

Ralph and Rebecca settled on the flat below Wainwright Hollow near the old Dry Saw Mill railroad station in 1812. We date Ralph and Rebecca's arrival here by an entry in Leonard

Morey's Journal when the Johnsons came up the Bennett's to settle near the mouth of Medix Run. The journal entry dated February 25, 1813, reads:

"Again moving up the river from Dent's, we reached a point near where Grant Station now is, and for the first time saw the cabin of Ralph Johnson. Ralph Johnson had come into this county during the fall previous and erected a shanty for his family (which he had just brought in before Morey and his party came up). Mr. Johnson remained here, building improvements in the way of mills and home"

As Morey has just explained, here Ralph cleared land, made improvements, and engaged in lumbering. In 1830, he built and operated a saw mill. His settlement became known as the Dry Saw Mill until sometime in the 1870's when President Grant came here on a fishing trip and the landing was renamed Grant.

Ralph and Rebecca had six children.

1. **Benjamin Johnson** - was born on July 4, 1813. He married Hannah Overturf (February 22, 1821- April 16, 1900). Benjamin and Hannah had five children: Luzerna M. married B.A. Booth, James Johnson married Hannah Apker, Hannah, Suzanne, and Florence M. who married Jean Bickel. Benjamin died March 9, 1886.

2. **M. Duke (Marmaduke) Johnson** born on March 31, 1814 - He married Massie (Martha) Overturf). He worked for his father until October 1845, when he married Massey Overturf, a daughter of Andrew and Hannah (Jordon) Overturf of Driftwood. They resided on a farm in Mt. Pleasant, known today as Winslow Hill. Mr. Johnson served as a township supervisor, together with holding various township offices. The family was members of the Methodist Episcopal Church. He died on September 17, 1890.

3. **Ann Johnson** (August 3, 1816 - October 10, 1874) married John Chaplian. They had three children: Jesse, Edith and Elliot.

4. **Thew Johnson** (February 14, 1817 - December 21, 1851)

5. **Jane Reed Johnson** - Born October 9, 1818, married Harrison Wilson

6. **Elizabeth Johnson** (June 25, 1820 - January 24, 1892)

married George Mahen

Rebecca died October 30, 1821. In 1825, Ralph remarried Margaret, the daughter of Frederick and Margretha (Grubb) Schaffer. Margaret was born in Pennsylvania on September 1801. They had eight children.

1. **John Johnson** (June 22, 1825 - December 27,xxxx) married daughter of Daniel & Mary (Heyemer) Miller on February 12, 1873.
2. **Simpson Johnson** (1827 - 1828)
3. **Ralph J. Johnson**, Jr. (May 27, 1828 - May 17, 1877, married twice, first
   Emily Wylie (Jan 10, 1834 - July 21, 1862)
   Maria Wainwright
4. **Edith (Edie) Johnson** (December 22, 1829 married Willard Bob Clark.
5. **Jesse Johnson** (October 23, 1831 - July 5, 1867)
6. **Emiline Johnson** (July 13, 1833 - March 24, 1883) married William Murray on June 9, 1853. They lived in Summerson, just north of junction of Route 555, and Winslow Hill Road.
7. **Amanda Johnson** (March 29, 1835-1906) married George Apker.
8. **David Summerson Johnson** (July 13, 1837 - December 21, 1906) married Adeline "Jemima" Overturf

Margaret died September 14, 1837, leaving Ralph a widower for the second time. Ralph remarried for a third time, to Hannah Jordon, who was born about 1792.

Ralph Johnson, one of Bennett's Branch's earliest settlers, made many contributions to the development of the area. He died at the age of 70 on September 14, 1837, and is buried next to his three wives, Rebecca, Margaret, and Hannah in the Johnson's Family Cemetery in Grant.

Thew Johnson Jr. 1795-1867

Thew Johnson Jr., was born in Yorkshire England in 1795. He came to the Bennett's Branch when he was about 22 years old in 1817. In 1822, Thew Jr. married Sarah Coleman and built a home in what is described as "The Windfall Bottoms". Here he engaged in farming and lumbering. Thew Jr.'s family, like his father, was also washed out in the disastrous flood of 1836,

Thew Johnson Jr.'s house in Grant that once served as an Inn
– Picture courtesy Johnson Family History by Eva Caylor

and, like his father, sought higher ground to relocate and build his second home. This was a rather large house and served for a number of years as Inn for the stagecoaches coming up and down the river from Lock Haven.

Years later when this house was being remodeled, a secret stairway leading to an obscure upstairs loft was discovered. A logical assumption is that this house served as a stopping point for the "Underground Railroad" for Negroes escaping from slavery in the South to freedom in Canada.

WILLIAM E. & ABIGAIL SOPHIA
JOHNSON
Picture courtesy of Virginia M. Hudsick

Thew Jr. and his wife Sarah had a family of nine children. Thew died in 1867. Sarah lived to be nearly ninety, passing away in May of 1889.

1. **ELIZA JOHNSON** - (1823-1843) married J.H. Goff.

SAMATHA JOHNSON
WINSLOW
Picture courtesy of
Virginia M. Hudsick

2.   **COLEMAN T. JOHNSON** - born about 1825 married Sarah H. Hicks

3.   **WILLIAM E. JOHNSON** - William E. Johnson, son of Thew Johnson Jr. and Sarah (Coleman) Johnson, was born November 6, 1826, in Elk Co. He spent his early life farming and lumbering. In1867, he established a general store, which he conducted until 1885. For sixteen years of that time he served as Postmaster of Benezette. In 1886 he moved to Punxsutawney, where he engaged in general merchandising until retiring in 1896. In 1851, he married Ann Murray, of Elk Co., who died in 1856, leaving one son, William S. (who lived in Punxsutawney). His second marriage was in 1858, to Abigail Sophia Winslow, daughter of Carpenter and Beulah (Keen) Winslow, natives of Maine. To his second marriage were born two daughters; Ella E., wife of William Zierden, of Johnsonburg, and Emma Pilk wife of Thaddeus C. Zeitler of Punxsutawney.

4.   **SAMATHA JOHNSON WINSLOW** – Born December 3, 1828.

5.   **JACOB E. JOHNSON** - Thew and Sara's oldest son, Jacob Johnson was born November 6, 1830, In Benezette Township and received his formal education in the common schools of Benezette. On May, 1856, Jacob married Margaret Murray of Benezette, a daughter of John and Hannah (Hollingworth) Murray. They raised three children: Alice (wife of Andrew Overturf); Everett B.; and Annie. Mr. Johnson had served Benezette Township in the capacity of Supervisor and School Director. The Johnsons were members of the Methodist Episcopal Church.

6.   **HARRIET JOHNSON** (born about 1832 married Stephen Wylie about 1832). They had one child - Sara Adeline born in or about 1860. Harriet had a second marriage to Mr.

Jonathan Osborn & Henrietta Johnson

Chatman

7. **JONATHAN OSBORN JOHNSON** - Born February 4, 1833, raised and educated in Benezette Township. Worked on the family farm until his marriage to Miss Henrietta Hollen, daughter of Thomas and Elizabeth (Overturf) on March 1, 1859. To Jonathan & Henrietta were born four children: W.B. Harriet, T.D. and Thomas. Henrietta died on July 10, 1869. In 1871, Jonathan remarried to Elvina A. Freeman daughter of Benjamin and Rebecca (Chandler) Freeman of Emporium, Pa. To this marriage were born five children: J.O., Ralph, Frank, Ella and Freeman. Mr. Johnson served Benezette Township in various official positions.

8. **NANCY ELLEN JOHNSON** - Born about 1835, she married Jacob Shaffer, a Benezette merchant, who was born at Sinnemahoning, Pa., on May 2, 1854, a son of Jacob L. and Nancy (Johnson) Shaffer, of German and Irish origin respectively. His grandparents were among the early settlers of Cameron and Elk Counties. After the completion of his education, Mr. Shaffer remained on the home farm until 1875, when he came to Benezette engaging with W.E. Johnson as clerk in his general store. He was married November 11, 1876, to Miss Belle M., a daughter of James F., and Emily (Barr) Thomas of Benezette, Penna., and they were blessed with five children: Mr. Shaffer was engaged in business for himself, as a lumberman and merchant, until June 30, 1884, when a disastrous fire caused by an exploded lamp in a store room, destroyed the entire business section and eleven houses. Shaffer's store and entire stock were burned to the ground in this fire, with a loss of $3,000.00 of the stock. He continued, however, in the lumber business until May 22, 1889, when he again opened a general store at Benezette. He had many adventures throughout his life and held various township offices. He was a member of Driftwood Lodge F & A.M. and Benezette Lodge I.O.O.F

9. **SARAH ELIZABETH JOHNSON** - Sara Elizabeth Johnson was born in or about 1839. She married Josiah Berfield, born January 9, 1831, died November 8, 1917. Sarah and Josiah Berfield, had eight children: Hugh, born in about 1859: Henry F., born in about 1863: Ellen, born about 1865; Elizabeth, born in about 1867; Orrel, born in about 1868; John Franklin, born October 30 1869; Thew J.

(December 25, 1858 - August 21, 1863), and Harriet (July 3, 1860 - August 3, 1863).

The Will of Thew Johnson, Jr., 1795-1867:

This is to certify that I, Thew Johnson, the undersigned testator, being of sound mind at the present time and not under influence from any person or persons whatever do make and revise the following as my last will and testament. First I bequeath to my two sons, Jacob Johnson and Jonathon Osborn Johnson, my farm on which I now reside with all the stock upon it and all the farming utensils, appertaining to be held by the said Jacob and Jonathon O. Johnson in equal shares. The above bequest is intended upon the following conditions. To wit, the said Jacob and Jonathon O. Johnson are to occupy the farm house, have the use of the stock and implements during my life and that of my wife of either or both of us and upon that event taking place, they are to come into full possession the farm in fee simple and the stock and farming tools as their own free from any encumbrance whatever. The conditions of the above are to be conditional. Namely, if the said Jacob and Jonathan O. Johnson shall fine a support for me and my family during life, we to reside in the house upon the farm where we now residing further shall pay to the following persons the following sums to Coleman Johnson three hundred dollars, William E. Johnson three hundred dollars, to Nancy Ellen Shaffer, two hundred and twenty five dollars, to Sarah Elizabeth Burfield, Two hundred and twenty five dollars and to Sarah Adeline Wylie, two hundred and twenty five dollars when she becomes of age if she lives and if not it will fall back to the rest of the   heirs. Further, I bequeath to Samantha Winslow, Nancy Ellen Shaffer and Sarah Elizabeth Burfield the beds and bedding and clothing belonging to the family the decease of myself and wife. This said Jacob and Jonathon O. Johnson will pay equal shares which will be seven hundred and fifty dollars and a lease. It is designed the above Jonathon O. Johnson shall occupy the house now standing on the above named farm as a permanent residence.

President Grant's Visit -1870's

Simon Cameron was Secretary of War when Grant was a general in the Union Army. Colonel Amos C. Noyes of Westport, Pa., was a large land owner and one of the most noted timber men on the West Branch of the Susquehanna. When Grant was president he was looking for an outdoor place to spend his vacation. The assumption is that Cameron introduced Grant to his friend Colonel Noyes, who suggested the trout streams on the Bennett's Branch. The President traveled in a private railroad car. He made an overnight stop at Colonel Noyes' home in Westport, and the next night traveled by train to Dry Saw Mill where the railroad had installed a siding in preparation for the President's visit. Grant's party fished in the headwaters of Mix Run and in Dent's Run which at the time were populated with numerous brook trout of which the Presidential party succeeded in catching several hundred. President Grant did not venture far from his car, but sat on the back platform smoking cigars and talking with the local people who gathered around to visit the president. We assume that some of the Johnsons had a visit with Grant, as he was camped out in their back yard. The railroad company changed the name of siding from Dry Mill Sawmill to Grant in honor of the President's visit

The Tree Bruin

December 19, 1887 - It appears that on that date, Ralph Johnson of Dry Saw-Mill, while in the woods about one mile from his house, stopped by the side of a large standing of Hemlock, when he heard, as he supposed, the breaking of ice, caused by his own weight, but a visual ray of about seven feet of his height proved to him that something with its head poked out of a small hole was gritting teeth within six inches of his boot. From the size of the hole, as it appeared from the outside of the tree, he though it an animal of some description, of inferior size, and blocked up the hole. Next morning, in company with John and Will Wainwright,

175

with two axes and an old rusty flintlock rifle that had seen better days was carried by Will, went to capture the prize, and to their surprise found a hollow larger than a flour barrel, which evidently had been lately vacated by an old bruin. They followed the trail about one mile and found him under a flat rock. Ralph, Will and the dog stood guard until John went and returned with two more guns, a double and single barrel rifle. Will fired first, but his dilapidated antique musket didn't do much more than give the bear a mild headache. However, a second shot fired from John's rifle was a fatal blow, striking the bear in the head. The boys had an exciting day, bagging a 200 pound bear as confirmed by the farm scale.

1847 and 1889 Floods

WALLACE H. JOHNSON, son of Simpson Johnson, was born on March 30, 1840, in Grant upon the farm cleared and settled by his grandparents - Thew & Ann Johnson. When Wallace was seven years of age, the flood of 1847 struck the Johnson homestead during the night with a devastating blow. Simpson awoke to find the house totally surrounded by fast moving flooding waters, and reacted to the immediate and impending danger by moving his wife and three children to higher ground in the barn loft. However, the surging waters were more devastating than initially thought, and set the barn floating down the turbulent flooded waters of the Bennett's Branch. The barn began to breakup leaving the family adrift and helplessly stranded on hay mow floor during this cold dark

WALLACE H. JOHNSON
Picture Courtesy of
Glen & Jane Mackey

night of unexpected disaster. The platform collided with a tree on the river's edge and Simpson somehow managed to get his family and himself up the tree to a point of temporary safety. They were rescued the second morning by someone on a raft. It was a hair raising experience for any family, but particularly for the young Wallace.

Wallace worked with his father on the family farm until June 4, 1864, when he married Emily Overturf, a daughter of Andrew and Elizabeth (Hess) Overturf. They raised a family of four children: Maggie, Mary F., Simpson, and Elizabeth. Emily died on February 1874, and the following December, Wallace married Mary Shaw - the widow of Richard Shaw, and daughter of Henry and Ann (Bounce) Rinker, of Philadelphia. Pa.

On June 1 & 2, 1889, there was another devastating flood on the Bennett's Branch which caused much damage to property and crops. Upon hearing that Lock Haven was hit hard with the flood and that supplies to the town were cut off as a result of the railroad bridges being washed out by the raging waters, Wallace became concerned for his daughter Maggie who lived in Lock Haven. Wallace and T.J. Shaffer, whose sister lived in Lock Haven, acquired a boat and supplies that included flour, ham, coffee, etc. and floated down the river to check on their situation. When he arrived Wallace found his daughter Maggie had survived the flood but one could only imagine that this flood brought back memories of the 1847 flood. When Wallace returned home, he found that his barn and contents together with all his out buildings had been destroyed by a fire of unknown origin.

Mr. Johnson built and operated a roller process grist mill with a capacity of thirty barrels of flour a day. Wallace Johnson held various township offices. He and his family were members of the Methodist Episcopal Church.

Disasters came without warning which left our ancestors with only one resolve: rebuild and make it better! The sandstone, slate, marble, and granite tombstones bear silent witness to their pioneer tenacity to clear the land, make a living, and raise their families in the primitive wilderness with the hope of having a better life.

END

Pennsylvania German Immigrants – 1709-1786
Genealogical Publishing Co., Inc. - Edited by Yoder
Democrat – Newspaper – by A. W. Gray
History of McKean, Elk, Cameron and Potter Counties, Penna Vol II – Beers
Andrew Overturf Research Notes from Branter/Anderson Research
History of Clearfield County
LPS Film #144923 – Tax Record, 1776-1796 for Snyder County
The Johnson story

ANTHONY BENEZET AND THE HISTORY OF BENEZETT(E)

Prior to the arrival of the white settlers to the Bennett's Branch, this was Seneca Indian Territory. There is enough circumstantial evidence to suggest that the plot of land upon which the village of Benezette is now located was once a Seneca Lodge, better known to the white man as a village. The Indian's name for

INDIAN MILL
Located on Little Medix Road

this place was Salt Lick, as there was a source of salt here. Windy Bloom once stated that the old timers referred to the road leading up to the Benezette Cemetery as Salt Lick Hill. The early settlers to the area found bark peeled from many standing trees, which the Indians cut to build huts called wigwams. Erasmus Morey said that when his family first came here Indian planting mounds were still visible. The Indians had a unique way of planting. They created a mound of soil, and planted mixed seeds, which usually included corn, squash, and pumpkins. The local citizens of Benezette have found a number of Indian artifacts in the form of arrowheads, stone axes, and pieces of pottery over the years.

When Sam Mc Kay surveyed the Second Fork in 1790, he noted the existence of an old cabin near the mouth of Trout Run. This was acknowledged as the cabin of John Bennett for whom the Second Fork would be renamed Bennett's Branch.

In the early 1800's, Benezette was called Potter's Flats, as General James Potter then owned this property. In 1815, Leonard

Morey purchased this land, consisting of a total of 379 ½ acres. Here he built a gristmill on a small tributary entering Trout Run and a large house, which served as an Inn for those passing up and down the branch, or for those needing to stay overnight who came to grind their grain at his mill.

Reuben and Ebenezer Winslow purchased this property from Morey in 1827. Reuben was a man of considerable energy and is acknowledged by most historians as being the founder of Benezette. He was also very active in local politics.

In the development of Pennsylvania as a Commonwealth, this area was once part of Northumberland County when this county was formed March 21, 1792. Later, on April 13, 1795, Lycoming County was carved from Northumberland, and still later on March 26, 1804, Benezette became part of Clearfield County. Between 1804 and 1807, Clearfield was annexed to Centre County. This was for the purpose of giving the citizens of Clearfield County a list of the taxable inhabitants. On April 18, 1843, Benezette became part of Elk County, being formed from a portion of Clearfield County.

As the county structure evolved, townships begin to develop within these counties. When Clearfield was formed in 1804, there was just one large township for the entire county by the name of Chinklasamoose Township. In 1813, this land became Lawrence Township, and later in 1817, Gibson Township, named after John Bannister Gibson, former Chief Justice of the Supreme Court and later Chief Justice of the Pennsylvania Supreme Court.

When Benezette Township was formed in February of 1846, Carpenter Winslow was elected Supervisor in the township's first election for officers. Reuben was Elk County's Commissioner at this time. Ever wonder where the name Benezette originated or why the founder of this community selected the name Benezette? This is a long story, but one worth telling as it is relates to the heritage of the area.

The French Connection: 12ᵗʰ Century

The ancient Province of Languedoc, France, begins at the West bank of the Rhone River and sweeps eastward to the border of Spain. The fertile soil of this province has produced lush grapes for twenty-five centuries. In the Cevennes Mountains, located within this province, there lived the family of Benoit. A son was born to this family in 1165, and during an eclipse of the sun in 1177, God spoke to this boy three times while he was alone tending his parents' flock of sheep. God told the boy that he was to leave his sheep, journey into Avignon, seek out the Bishop and tell him that he would build for God, a bridge across the Rhone River.

Walk With an Angel

The Boy spoke to God saying he had neither education nor money. God told him that he had nothing to fear, that He would show him how to build the bridge, and the people would freely donate the money. When the boy told God that he did not know the way to the Rhone and Avignon, God supplied him with an angel, disguised as a traveler, to lead him there. When the angel and the boy reached the Rhone River, across from Avignon, the angel reminded him that he had nothing to fear and vanished.

The boy persuaded a boatman to ferry him across the river. In the city he found the Bishop and his entourage. The Bishop was addressing a crowd. The boy spoke to the Bishop and the crowd, telling them that God had sent him to build a bridge across the Rhone. The crowd laughed and mocked him. They told him that many learned persons had tried to bridge the river and failed, that he was nothing but a penniless, crazy boy. As he persisted, the leader of the entourage threatened to skin him alive and cut off his feet.

Saint Benezet 1165-85

To show God had willed him, he picked up a large boulder that would have taken several men to lift and carried it like a pebble to the bank of the river. As he deposited it in the river, he announced, "This is where I will build a bridge for God." Then he went among the crowd and with God's powers he made the blind see, the mute speak, the deaf to hear and the lame walk.

Witnessing these miracles, eighteen in all, the crowd knelt down and praised him, called him a son of God and a saint. They named him Saint Benezet due to his age and small stature. (Benezet is a diminutive of Benoit.) The crowd arose and freely donated the money to start the construction of the bridge.

St. Benezet drew up the plans and started construction of the stone and cement bridge. During 1185, at the tender age of 20 and before the bridge was completed, God called him home. The bridge builders had idolized St. Benezet. They erected a tomb on the bridge and laid him in it. 500 years later, part of the bridge was damaged during a flood. His tomb was opened, and the people found his body intact. Today, St. Benezet's relics are at St. Didler's.

Before his death, St Benezet had a hospital built where he founded the religious order of Les Freres du Pont. He is revered throughout France and recognized by the Catholic Church in a litany that offers its petition to him as "ears of the deaf, speech of the mutes, sight of the blind, patron of the city of Avignon, and refuge against the floods of the Rhone". He is also the patron saint of an engineering college in Paris.

Today, 800 years later, part of the bridge span and foundation still stand, having weathered the destructive forces of both nature and man. The bridge that God willed an uneducated shepherd boy to build is honored in song and is a pilgrimage site. The son of a Benoit, who would be named St. Benezet, is apparently the first Benezet, 1165-1185.

The Huguenot Massacres 1572

In the later half of the sixteenth century, France was almost in constant civil and religious turmoil between the Catholics and the protestants, who would later become known as the Huguenots. Catherine de Medici, mother of King Charles IX, and former Queen of France, gave secret orders to her son, the King, on St. Bartholomew Day, September 24, 1572, to get rid of the problem, and massacre the Huguenots. There were thousands of Huguenots killed, causing many families to flee their homeland in France. This included the John Benezet family. This family, although Huguenots are connected to St. Benezet, is obviously Catholic by the surname – Benezett.

Refuge in Holland 1700's

Stephan Benezet married Judith de la Mejenelle October 29, 1709. She was a beautiful Huguenot lady who had served in the courts of French noblemen. Due to the faithful service that John Stephan's father had rendered to the government, as well as Judith's connections with nobility, they were able to escape persecution longer than other Huguenots. However, when they learned their holdings and estates were to be seized by the French government, they fled for Rotterdam, Holland, some 170 miles away. At the border a guard accepted their bribe of gold and let them pass to freedom. This man, his pregnant wife, a four year old daughter and a two year old son, started their winter overland trek on February 3, 1715, and arrived in Rotterdam February 15, 1715.

Rotterdam-Greenwich-Philadelphia 1715-1731

The family lived with relatives for six months and then left for Greenwich England, August 22, 1715. They arrived August 26, 1715. After a month in Greenwich, the family moved to London, England, where John either started a merchants business or worked for his Uncle Jacques. They remained in this general area until 1731, when they left England and entered America through the Port of Philadelphia, Pennsylvania.

While living in England, John and some members of his family embraced the Quaker (Friends) belief. After he arrived in Philadelphia, he attended services at Christ Church, Episcopalian, Church of England. Later John joined the Moravian faith and attended the First Moravian Church that once stood on Race and Bread Streets.

John and Judith established their home at 2nd and Quarry Street, a street which no longer exist. In 1746, they relocated to a home in Germantown, in Philadelphia County. There currently exists today a street named Benezet in Germantown that was more than likely named in his honor.

Spreading Wealth and Knowledge: A Quaker Tradition

In Philadelphia, a Quaker city of Brotherly Love, John became a successful merchant and apparently a man of wealth as he purchased "hundreds of acres" of land in the city and county. In Germantown he was named trustee of the "New Building," given to the "Academy" during 1749. The September 12, 1751, edition of the Pennsylvania Gazette reported that the New Building would be opened on September 16th as a free school for the poor. The Academy would later be named the College of Pennsylvania, and in turn, the University of Pennsylvania. Records indicate that John Stephan was a trustee of the college and university.

During the years 1741-46, John made several trips to Bethlehem, Pennsylvania, in the interest of his Moravian Brothers. He established a wayside house for mail carriers and teamsters going to and from Bethlehem. John and Judith both died in their Germantown home. John died April 1, 1751. Judith died at the age of 72 on September 4, 1765. They are buried in Old Hood's Cemetery, Logan and Germantown Avenue, Philadelphia, Pa.

Anthony (Anthoine) Benezet, the third born child of John & Judith Benezet, was born at St. Quentin, France, January 31, 1713, and died in Philadelphia, Pennsylvania, May 3, 1784. Anthony married Joyce Marriot (Joice Marrriott) of Burlington, New Jersey, March 13, 1736. A vast amount has been written about Anthony in early encyclopedias of Philadelphia, three separate biographies, and other books. He became a member of the Friends (Quaker) faith in England. Joyce was also a Quaker and together they were active in Friends meetings and their causes. They moved to Wilmington, Delaware, where Anthony became a merchant. However, dissatisfied with that occupation they returned to Philadelphia where Anthony became an educator. He is credited with founding what is known as the William Penn Charter School; starting the first high school for the poor girls in Germantown; and opening the first school to educate Negroes of all ages. He donated his service to the Negroes' school, willed a substantial amount of money to the Friends to maintain the school, and during the 200th celebration of Freedom in 1976, a nationally syndicated columnist termed him the "Martin Luther King of the 1700's. Anthony also championed the cause of the Indians, was a pacifist who believed that all differences could be settled without bloodshed, was a deadly foe of slavery; and was a philanthropist who for forty years generously gave daily bread to hungry people.

Choosing a Name

When the Commissioners of Elk County formed townships within the county on December 18, 1845, the Township was first spelled Benezet. When the township was officially formed in February of 1843, subsequent documents refer to the spelling as "Benezet". A logical assumption would be that the township was named after the village of Benezet. Who selected this name for the village or when this name was selected is not known.

There was a question addressed to a newspaper in Williamsport a number of years ago: "A town and township in Elk Co., Pa., are called Benezette. What is the origin of the name?" F.B.

The answer:

The town of Benezette, established in 1844, was named after Alonzo Benezet or his son Ralph, descendants of Huguenot refugees who had settled in Philadelphia early in the 18th century. Three families, the Mowreys, the Winslows and the Bennetts, who were early settlers in the section Elk Co. in which Benezette is now situated, were having trouble deciding on a name for their town when Alonzo Benezet moved there from Philadelphia where he had been a tutor to Quakers. Apparently he and his family created a fine impression for the town was named and first spelled Benezett, also the township. The U.S. Post Office still used that spelling but the residents use Benezette.

Alonzo Benezet, a descendant of Anthony Benezet, was born October 23, 1858. Anthony did not have a son named Ralph, but he did have a nephew named Ralph. Anthony Benezet was born in New Jersey, January 4, 1875. The dates would rule out these two individuals from the considerations of having the town named after them for the reason of local residence. There isn't any evidence to support that a family of Benezet ever lived here.

Benezette could have been named after Philip, John, Stephen, or Anthony Benezet. The Benezette family hasn't been able to determine how the town got its name despite all the research and information gathered to date. There are various theories or ideas. The most logical assumption would be Anthony and the principles, which he represented. In any event, the Benezets did make their mark on this young country during their lifetime, and bequeathed to future generations of citizens a moral standard that many people of all faiths and nationalities would be proud to emulate.

Local Lore

Local residents once claimed that the town received its name when two boys, one who stuttered, the other named Ben, ventured into the nearby forest. A bear attacked the boys, and dragged Ben off. The other boy ran to town screaming and stuttering – Ben-is-ate, Ben-is-ate, supposedly giving the village its name. This story was more than likely perpetrated upon the local citizens by some fun loving wood-hick. Told over and over again, it became part of the local folk lore.

Benezette

Most of us have experienced some variation in the spelling of our surnames over the past few centuries, especially following immigration. The same change is true for many of our towns. So is the case of BENEZETTE. The spelling of Benezet over the years evolved to Benezette, as did the spelling of the neighboring town Medoc Run to Medix Run. The U. S. Post Office's official designation of the community is Benzett, but the vast majority of the local citizens and many of the descendants of Anthony Benezet spell the name BENEZETTE.

The village of Benezette has thrived over the years as a lumbering outpost upon the river highway, a link in the underground railroad, a bastion of ghost stories and the lost gold shipment lore, and is now a thriving mecca for elk and tourists.

THE END

History of McKean, Elk, Cameron and Potter Counties – Vol. II by Beers
The Benezette Genealogy as prepared by Fred C. Benezette and Frank E. Benezette, Jr.
The Elk Horn – Elk County Historical Society – Vol 33 – Winter issue 1997
Bennetts Valley News Paper – March 13, 2003
Journal of Samuel MaClay Published by John F. Meginness,
WENNAWOODS PUBLISHING

RR2 Box 529c Goodman Road
Lewisburg, Pennsylvania
www.wennawoods.com.

THE DEN(N)ISONS

DENISON HOMESTEAD MUSEUM
Built in 1717 by George Denison on land granted to his grandfather Captain
George Denison, one of Mystic's earliest settlers. Each room, furnished with
Denison heirlooms, depicts a different period in American history. Picture
courtesy of the Denison Society.

Starr Dennison and Spring Run

The Denison's family pioneering history in the early westward
expansion of North America is of a magnitude to rival the heroic
deeds of such famous American pioneer explorers as Daniel Boone
and Jim Bridger. From the day in 1627, when the first Denison set
foot on the North American Continent, to Starr Dennison's arrival
in Spring Run to settle, the Denison pioneering legacy presents a
very interesting story in the annals of early American History.

The War of 1812 extinguished nearly all the Indian hostilities in Pennsylvania, although some friendly Seneca Indians still roamed the mountains and stream beds in the Bennett's Valley area. About this same time the New Holland Land Company began to sell off their land holdings in Western Pennsylvania. This is the same land they had acquired in the treaty of Big Tree known as the 1784-5 "Last Purchase." This land sale opened this territory to the westward marching settlers.

In March of 1818, Starr Dennison and his family migrated from their home in Mayfield, New York, to become one of the first, if not the first, family to settle in the Spring Run area.

From England 1630

Starr's ancestry dates back earlier than the 14th century when the Dennisons were granted their coat-of arms with heraldry symbols of a Crusader and naval service.

Denison

Starr's first ancestor to come to America was William Dennison, who migrated with his family from Stortford, England, to Roxbury, Connecticut, in 1630-31. Joining William were his wife, Margaret Chandler, and sons Daniel and George. The Dennison family of four departed on the risky and arduous two month ocean crossing for New England on the ship *Lion* which sailed in a fleet of sixteen other ships, part of what was called the Winthrop Fleet. This was the first large armada of newcomers which quickly multiplied the population of New England and stabilized the tenuous population of the villages. The floodgate of immigrants was opened.

William was a prominent and prosperous citizen of Stortford where he owned and operated malt houses. The primary reasons for William leaving England were to escape religious persecution along with an alarming concern of recurring plagues in England, one of which had claimed the life of his father.

William, now free of England's religious intolerance, became the founder and deacon of the First Church in Roxbury, Massachusetts. Through his diligence and previous business acumen, William soon became a prosperous merchant and ship-owner in his adopted country.

William's son Daniel became head of the Massachusetts Militia as a major general and aide to the governor. Daniel also helped in the founding of the town of Ipswich.

William's son, George Denison, Starr's direct ancestor, would make a number of noble contributions to the peoples, both white and red, as a pioneer settler and explorer with military service and political leadership.

George Dennison- a Fearless Independent

George was about eleven years old when he migrated to Roxbury, Mass. with his father. He received his formal education from John Eliot, a distinguished missionary to the Indians of the New England area. At the age of 22, George married Bridget Thompson, a very popular young lady of the Roxbury settlement. They had two daughters: Sarah and Hannah.

Sadly, three years following their marriage, George was dealt a devastating blow when Bridget unexpectedly died. George, distraught over her death, and having a habit of making quick decisions, almost immediately following Bridget's funeral services, left his two young daughters with his mother-in-law, and galloped to Boston. Here he booked passage on the first ship sailing for England to join Oliver Cromwell's army against the Royalist Forces of King Charles.

In England, George took his training quite seriously and engaged in a number of skirmishes. His dedication to duty and bravery in battle soon advanced him to the rank of Captain. He distinguished himself in several battles but was severely wounded late in the war when a musket ball struck him in the shoulder.

George's uncle, Edward Denison, William's brother, had been appointed Deputy Governor with headquarters in York. Edward arranged for his wounded nephew to recover from his battle wound at the home of John Borodell, a well to do merchant in leather wares. John's daughter Ann, known by family and friends as Lady Ann, served as George's nurse. While recovering from his wound, George and Lady Ann fell in love and were married.

With the Cromwell War nearly over, George, in June of 1646, returned to Roxbury with his new wife Lady Ann and was greeted with a hero's welcome and admitted as freeman of the town.

In Roxbury, George reunited with his daughters whom he had left behind when he went off to war in England. The family established residence on a 500 acre farm. For the next four years, he kept busy tending to his family and farm. Here on July 14, 1646, George and Lady Ann's first son, John, was born. On May 20, 1649, they were blessed with a second child whom they named Ann.

While in Roxbury, George became very concerned and strongly felt that the local militia was not adequate to fight off a united Indian attack against the settlement. In 1650, knowing the need for a stronger militia and feeling that his experience in the Cromwell War made him qualified, he ran for the position of Commander of the Train Band, the local militia. He lost the election by a very narrow margin.

Frustrated over losing this important election, George turned to his old tutor, the missionary minister John Eliot for council and advice. John Eliot spent much of his time traveling and spreading the word of the gospel among the neighboring Indian tribes. Eliot had relations with the Narragansetts, Wampanoags, Moghegans, Pawtuckets, Massachusetts, Hassamanicos, and Nipmucks, and sincerely felt that converting the Indians to Christianity was an important step in establishing peaceable relations in the territory.

Eliot, after listening to George's concerns about the Indians, suggested that George accompany him on his next missionary trip. George immediately recognized this as an opportunity to learn about Indians and the lands outside the borders of the settlements. That fall the two men set out on a missionary trip into Indian Territory.

Eliot introduced George to the Indians as a great warrior, while representing himself as a man of the cloth. Their first stop was a visit with Narragansetts where they were well received. As they continued on the journey, George quickly learned the Indian language as well the universal sign language. He made a number of positive and friendly relations with most of the sachems, chiefs, and tribal leaders. Among these friends were included Chief Onceco and Unicas who were made famous by James Fennimore Cooper's novel, "The Last of the Mohicans".

While on this trip, George confirmed his belief that the colonies' militias could not defend themselves against an attack of a united coalition of Indian tribes. He saw for himself that the Indians could fire ten metal tipped arrows with deadly accuracy in the same time it would take a militiaman to load and fire one of their fuse burning muskets. He also learned a united coalition among all the tribes would be a very uncomfortable union for both sides.

While George and John were venturing beyond the frontier of Connecticut, they paid a visit to the wilderness trading post of Thomas Stanton on Pawcatuck. Stanton had an excellent reputation among both the Indians and settlers as being a fair trader. A strong friendship soon developed between George and Stanton. The Pawcatuck country held a strong attractive appeal to George. Stanton, learning of George's military background and frustrations with the Massachusetts Colony, encouraged him to move to Connecticut, an idea, which George found interesting.

During their stay with Stanton, George and John learned that the Pequots were endeavoring to form an alliance with the Narragansetts to attack the white settlers. Since the Narragansetts' village was on their return route home, and they seemed to have created good relations on their initial visit there, George and John decided to pay them a second visit. What they found was alarming. The rumor was true. The Pequots were attempting to form a coalition with the Narragansetts to attack the white settlements. John Eliot's friendship with the Indians was about to save many lives. Eliot and George were able to persuade the Narragansetts of their peaceable intentions and to reject the Pequots proposed alliance to make war on the settlements, thus avoiding a bloody conflict.

Upon returning home to Roxbury, George decided to pay a visit to his brother, Daniel, who was General of the Massachusetts Militia. George explained to Brother Dan the role he and John Eliot played in avoiding a conflict with the Indians and the need to build a stronger militia for adequate protection of the colonies. Daniel, for various political reasons, turned a deaf ear on George's plea.

George, realizing his ideas in Massachusetts were unwelcomed, moved to New London, a frontier outpost settlement in Connecticut. Although their new home in New London did not offer the same quality of life as Roxbury, and caused many hardships on the Denison family, it did offer George the freedom to develop his ideas for a strong militia. George erected makeshift living quarters for his family and began clearing land for a farm on the rich soil. Soon after arriving he assumed command of the town's militia. He developed a training manual based on his previous military experience, adapted it for Indian warfare, and gradually began training a well organized militia.

About three years after moving to New London, lands for settlement opened up in the Mystic area near the vicinity of Stanton's trading post. These lands, about six miles from George's current residence, could best be described as an outpost settlement to the frontier settlement of New London. This had a special appeal for George who believed this remote location offered much opportunity and independence for adventurous and daring men. So once again the Denison family moved, this time to an even more primitive area.

George erected crude living quarters for his family in Mystic on the edge of the civilized country, and once again, took to clearing land for a farm. Soon after George's arrival, more settlers began to move into the area, creating the small settlement known as Stonington. For both political and religious reasons, Stonington was attached to New London. The social structure of the day required settlers to regularly attend church every Sunday. The trail from Stonington to New London, although only six miles long, required a traveler to cross both the Mystic and Thames Rivers causing a difficult journey for a family.

The settlers of Stonington twice petitioned the colony of Connecticut for the right to form their own township, but their requests were denied. George decided to petition the Massachusetts Colony to have Stonington annexed to their colony. This was an idea that appealed to Massachusetts, but upset Connecticut, and caused a heated disagreement between the two colonies. The matter was decided by the Colonial Committee who re-established the boundary between the two colonies at the Mystic River, making Stonington part of the Massachusetts Colony. Needless to say, this didn't make the Connecticut Colony very happy.

George assumed a leadership role in the new township and attained the authority to perform marriages and set boundary lines, along with all the responsibilities of a community leader. For the next four or five years things seemed to be functioning very well within the settlement until King Charles II of England reset the boundary to its original position, thus returning Stonington back to the Connecticut Colony.

The political leaders of the Connecticut Colony, once Stonington was returned to their Colony, began a revengeful retaliation against George for his role in instigating the controversy. They leveled a special tax on the settlers in Stonington and tried to strip George of his political authority in the new township.

George, frustrated with the situation, refused to pay their fines, and continued to perform various community functions such as marriages. In addition, George challenged the Connecticut authorities with a number of issues and rebelled against the establishment. While all this commotion was going on, the King Philip War erupted.

King Philip War 1675

In the early 1600's, Metacom succeeded his father Massasoit as Grand Sachem of the Wampanoag. Metacom, called King Philip by the colonists vowed to stop the erosion of Indian lands to the colonists, and formed an alliance with Chief Canonchet of the Narragansetts. In June of 1675, the war began when the Indians attacked the village of Swansey, killing about 9 settlers, and burning most of the village to the ground. The war quickly spread throughout the New England area with a dreadful outcome. Over 90 colony settlements were attacked and a large number of settlements were wiped out. 600 to 800 settlers and over 3000 Indians were killed over the next two years.

After some political wrangling, George entered the war. George's war experience in Cromwell's War, coupled with his knowledge of the local Indian tribes and the alliances he and Stanton maintained with Indians friendly to the white settlers, would play an important role in the outcome of this war. The Pequots, Mohegans, and Niantics were all active allies. George welded an effective fighting unit to meet the challenge against the warring tribes. Under George's leadership, his force made a number of successful attacks on Narragansett villages, inflicting devastating consequences to the Indians. George's militia captured Chief Canonchet. He was given the choice of laying down his arms against the colonists or execution. The Chief chose execution and was beheaded.

George's success against the Indians spread throughout the New England settlements. He was praised for both his foresight and accomplishments in the King Philip's war. The governor appointed him as a fully accredited deputy to the General Court in Hartford. In addition he was given a considerable amount of land by both Connecticut and the Pequots.

George also was instrumental in negotiating the first American Indian Reservations, and while the Indians considered George to be very fair with them, the reservations were not very popular with the settlers.

As an interesting note, according to the old records from Mansfield, Conn., Kenelm Winslow, (also profiled in this book), bought from George Denison, of Stonington, one thousand acres of land in Windham, in that part of the town which afterwards became Mansfield, Connecticut.

In the old village of Stonington near where George Denison once endured the hardships of pioneer life, together with dealing with the local American Indians, stands the Denison Homestead Museum. Built in 1717, by George's ancestors, this homestead, now located on the Pequotsepos Road in Mystic, Connecticut, was continuously owned and lived in by the Denison family for six generations. This museum is furnished entirely with Denison Family Heirlooms and allows visitors a glimpse into the life of an American farm family encompassing five different periods of American History.

MAYFLOWER DESCENDENTS

One of Starr's direct ancestors was William Brewster, making Starr's family Mayflower descendants. William Brewster was a Pilgrim leader who established Plymouth Colony in 1620. He was the only member of the Pilgrim Fathers to have some university training, having studied briefly at Cambridge in England. Brewster was the church's ruling elder in the Plymouth Colony and shared with William Bradford and Edward Winslow in the leadership of the Plymouth enterprise. Starr's ancestry can be traced back to his grandfather Daniel, then on to Mary Wetherall, Grace Brewster,

Jonathan Brewster, and then to the first governor and leader of the Plymouth Colony – William Brewster. Somewhere between William's arrival in America and Starr's family, the spelling of the family name evolved from Denison to Dennison.

STARR DENNISON

Starr Dennison was born in New London, Connecticut on April 16, 1771, the son of Thomas and Katherine Starr Dennison. Starr moved with his father in 1800, to Mayfield, New York. While living in Mayfield, Starr married the Connecticut born Chloe Stone and together they had five children: Asenith (b 1801), Vine (b 1803), Daniel (born 1804), Starr Jr. (b 1806) and Jeremiah (born 1812). In addition there was a sixth child, Chloe born in Pennsylvania in 1824.

When the Dennison family came from Mayfield, New York, to settle in Spring Run, we assume they followed the same route taken by the Morey Family when they arrived in 1813 to settle in Medix Run. This journey would start in the vicinity of Towanda, New York, and then follow the waterways to Williamsport. Here they probably hired boatsmen to ferry them up the river in canoes, perhaps as far as the Dutchman's cabin at the mouth of Second Fork, or maybe all the way up the fork to Dr. Rogers', New Holland's land agent's, cabin in Summerson. We surmise, based upon family stories handed down from generation to generation that they came with oxen which would have to be driven up the Indian trails along the river banks. Once they reached the present location of Benezette, they would follow a trail from the mouth of Trout Run to the headwaters of Spring Run where Stony Brooks enters the stream. Here they built a cabin establishing themselves as pioneer settlers. The land upon which they settled is presently owned by Gary Chase, a Dennison descendant.

In 1843, when Elk County was formed, and later in 1843 when Jay Township came into existence, the Dennisons played a role in the development of both the county and township. Starr,

Jr. replaced Thomas Dent as Commissioner of Elk County and later, in 1849, he ran as a Wig and was elected Elk County Auditor. The taxpayer records of township indicate Vine Dennison as owning a sawmill.

Joseph Burke told the story about the Dennison lost coins. Vine Dennison lived on what is now Mc Clintick Road, on the old Dill estate. Before Vine died, he claimed to have buried coins across the road within the sight of his house. Vine had written a poem describing where the coins were buried. My grandfather once had a copy of this poem, but the copy of the poem has disappeared. However, when the poem was read to me when I was very young, I remember the mention of a hedge row and a large pine tree. My grandfather was hired to plow the field in search of the coins, but to my knowledge the coins were never found.

Starr Dennison's Family Cemetery plot.

Starr Dennison died on June 18, 1844. His wife Chloe died at the age of 84 on January 30, 1865. They are buried in an unattended family grave site near the foot of Smith Road, in Spring Run. The head stones are badly in need of repair, and hopefully someday this will become a historical site honoring the pioneer heritage of the Den(n)ison family.

THE END

Starr Dennison's Family Cemetery plot.

Editor's note: The Mt. Zion Historical Society will give $100.00 to the first person to give them an authentic copy of Vine Dennison's poem.

CREDITS INCLUDE

History of McKean, Elk, Cameron and Potter Counties – Beers

Captain of Destiny – by Ray W. Denison

Westward to Destiny – by Ray W. Denison
Captain George & Lady Ann – by Willilams Haynes
The Denison Society Inc.
King Philip's War by Eric B. Schultz and Michael J. Tougias
Plymouth Mass. – Its History & People
The Genealogy of William A. Winslow and Gladys M. Burke – by Butch Nay

BROOKINS FAMILY

CHARLIE BROOKINS

The Brookins' family history as here presented is a hypothetical encounter involving several of Bennett's Valley's most distinguished forefathers - Frederick Weed, his son-in-law, Erasmus Morey, and Charlie Brookins. For this imagery episode, we turn the clock of time back to 1836. The scene begins with Fredrick and Erasmus and their wives, Nancy and Mary, traveling in their horse-drawn carriage down a dusty road in Spring Run late one Sunday afternoon to visit Charles and Betsy Brookins who live on what we know today as

ELIJAH BROOKINS- Son of Charles and Betsey Brookins, and husband of Harriet Gardner, daughter of S.R. & Phoebe Pearsall Gardner. Rendering done by Lynda Pontzer.

the Old Dodge Road. The purpose of Frederick and Erasmus' excursion to visit Brookins, besides a friendly visit, is to invite the family to a Fourth of July Celebration.

Erasmus's brother-in-law, Richard Geolott, was making a number of plans for a grand Fourth of July celebration to be held at Richard's home in Medoc Run, a place we know today as Medix Run. In preparation for this event, Richard had built an outdoor pavilion, a liberty pole, and several flag poles. In addition, Richard had made arrangements for several guest speakers who most likely included Frederick Weed and Pvt. Isaac Webb, both veterans of the Revolutionary War who lived in the valley. There were also preparations for games and other entertainment to celebrate the birth of our new nation. This was a big event, undoubtedly the biggest event of the year on the Bennett's Branch.

Upon our visitors' arrival to the Brookins' farm, they were cordially greeted by both Charlie and Betsy, and after exchanging some pleasantries, Betsy invited Nancy and Mary into the parlor for some tea and sugar cookies and women talk. Charlie invited Frederick and Erasmus to join him around a small campfire, near his wagonshed in the rear of the premises for some men talk. Placed around the fire were some hand hewed log benches, that Charlie's son George had crafted, and while the guests were taking up residence on the benches, Charlie fetched a jug of corn whiskey that he had been saving for a special occasion from the shed. Just before he sat down, he handed the jug to Fredrick, and threw a couple of small logs on the fire and joined them on one of the benches. As the three of them, facing the fire, began jawboning about what was going on up and down the Valley, Frederick explained to Charlie about the Fourth of July Celebration and extended to him and Betsy an invitation to attend. Charlie seemed pleased to be asked, and said, "Thank you very much. You bet your boots that both Betsy and I will be there" Now that the Fourth of July celebration was discussed their conversation turned to the revolution, George Washington, and the many sacrifices their fathers and grandfathers had made in giving this nation its freedom. Charlie listened as both Frederick and Erasmus told various stories. Erasmus mentioned about attending George Washington's funeral services with his parents when he was just a young boy. Erasmus asked Frederick about some of his experiences in the war, and Frederick told some amusing stories about his Captain Schofield and a bit about fighting the Red Coats at Stamford. Erasmus asked his father-in-law about being a member of the Washington Benevolent Society of Saratoga, when Frederick interrupted him to ask Charlie if any of the Brookins fought in the war.

Charlie, who had been quietly and intently listening to their stories while staring into the embers of the glowing fire, replied, "Yeap", as he looked up, "you see that there bear skin over there tacked to the shed wall?" Of course, this was obvious and they both acknowledged the skin. "I shot that bear with the musket that my daddy carried in the War," Both Frederick and Erasmus became extremely curious and wanted to hear more. "Well", said Charlie, "it is a long story," as he began to tamp some tobacco into an old clay pipe he had taken from his shirt pocket, "but if you're interested," I'll tell you about the Brookins Story."

Charley went on to tell the following story.

"Well, boys", Charlie said, "since you asked, the first of us Brookins to come to this country was John, back in 1658, I believe."

Erasmus asked, "Did he come from England?"

"Yeap," Charlie replied, "he was a staunch Puritan from a place called Tolnes. He came over with a bunch of those Puritans folks and settled in Boston."

Frederick pointed out, "Those Puritans sure did have some strange ideas burning people they thought were witches and all."

"They sure did," Charlie said, "but the Brookins didn't have any part of that nonsense." "John run a place called the Salutation Inn in Boston," Charlie said, "and got himself married to a woman by the name of Elizabeth Holland."

Erasmus spoke, "Salutation Inn. That is a strange name for an Inn."

"Sure is," replied Charlie. "They say it got its name from a painted sign that hung on the front of the place showing a little boy saluting a girl."

Charlie continued on as Frederick and Erasmus listened intently: "You know back in those days an inn keeper was a man of influence with almost as much prestige in the settlement as the town elder. People would come to him for advice, and sometimes to borrow money or other favors, and in addition he was usually the first person in the settlement to hear all the current affairs and gossip. It wasn't uncommon for the inn keeper of a settlement to serve as the local school teacher, and to lead the singing in church."

Frederick, commented, "Ain't like it is today,"

"Let me tell you, boys," Charlie said, "John did quite well for himself over his lifetime. When he died, he owned a lot of land in and around Boston. About eight or nine years after he died, his wife Elizabeth sold the inn to the Governor of the Province, a man named Sir William Phipps".

Erasmus said, "The Salutation Inn. That name rings a bell, but I just cannot seem to put my finger on it."

SIR WILLIAM PHIPS
Govenor of the Massachuestts Bay Colony
5-16-1692 to 11-17-1694
Picture from Wikipedia

"Well, it should," replied Charlie. "The Inn got to be a well known place. About eighty years after Elizabeth sold the place, Sam Adams and Warren, together with a bunch of other rebel rousing patriots of the times met there to promote support for the Revolution. They called themselves the North Caucus or Sons of Liberty," I tell you, it was here, in this inn that Old Sam and the boys got the idea to dress up like some Indians and throw some tea into Boston Harbor."

"Yeap, I remember now," Frederick said. "That Boston Tea Party sure got a lot of things stirred up."

"Well anyway," said Charlie, "the old Salutation Inn became quite a historical landmark."

"Sure did," Frederick replied.

Charlie went on telling the Brookins Story: "About 1700, John's youngest son William moved his family from Boston to

Marlboro to settle. William's young son, Philip, was my great grand daddy who grew up in Marlboro during a time when there was still a good deal of turmoil and trouble with the Indians. The Stonebridge Indians who lived near the settlement were generally very friendly, but them darn French would stir up roving bands of Canadian Indians to raid the English settlements. These renegades would often raid settlements, murdering and scalping the men, and taking women and children captives. Sometimes the Indians would ransom the captives back to the settlement, but most often in these cases they were never heard of again. Some times the women, and even some of the kids, ransomed back to the settlement would run off back to their Indian friends for whatever reason."

Erasmus asked, "Was your ancestors ever hurt or harmed by the Indians?"

"Not to my recollection, but just before Philip and his dad arrived in Marlboro, a woman by the name of Mary Howe decided to visit her sister in the neighboring settlement of Lancaster when she was captured by the Indians and dragged off to Canada. Several years later she was ransomed back to the Marlboro Settlement and married the Deacon Thomas Keyes, to whom she was engaged at the time of her capture. Mary lived on to the ripe old age of eighty-nine, and over her lifetime just the mere mention of the word Indian would set her off in a frantic frenzy as a result of her horrific experience of being captured by them savages years ago.

"Now then, when Phillip was just a boy in Marlboro, two other boys were captured by the Indians."

"Whatever happened to them?" asked Erasmus.

"Now that an interesting story, Erasmus," Charlie replied, "From what I heard, years later the settlers of Marlboro learned that these same two boys became Indian chiefs and completely severed their ties with their white kinfolk."

Frederick said, "That is a bit strange."

Charlie continued on with the Brookin's Story. "When Philip became twenty-one he married a girl from the neighboring town of Lancaster."

"Who did he marry Charlie?" asked Frederick.

"He got pretty lucky. He snagged on a girl by the name of Sarah Keys. Her old man was John Keys who was among the most wealthy and prominent men in both Lancaster and Marlboro. Hell, John was a leading man in most all of the local religious and community affairs," said Charlie.

"Now in 1741," said Charlie, "Philip, like his father, got itchy feet, so he and a number of other families from Marlboro and Lancaster decided to move on. Being a younger group they wanted a place where they could govern themselves rather than be governed by the old elders of Marlboro."

"Were did they move to?" asked Erasmus.

"Well, they moved over to Western Massachusetts in Berkshire County and founded a settlement they called New Marlboro. Here in New Marlboro they lived within a short distance of a tribe of Stockbridge Indians."

"Were these Indians friendly?" , inquired Frederick.

"Oh yes." replied Charlie. "They were an off chute of the Mohicans, whom the settlers renamed Stockbridge because many of them lived near the settlement of Stockbridge, Maine. In any event they did build a fort on Leffingwall Hill for protection, probably from those Indians allied with the French."

Charlie continued on with the Brookin's Story: "The first native white residents of New Marlboro were a set of twins born to Philip and Sarah. My granddad, Cyrus, often would joke that his Mom was as fertile as the Nile River, because Pa always kept her knocked-up. Philip and Sara had seventeen sons."

Erasmus exclaimed, "Wow that a big family".

Charlie, with a grin, said, "That ain't nothin, Remember the guy I told you about who bought the Inn – Sir William Philip? He was reported to have twenty-six children, all boys. Some say, but I find it hard to believe that all of them had the same mother."

Charlie continued, "In 1771, Cyrus and two of his brothers, along with several other families of New Marlboro moved still further west to Vermont and there founded the town of Poultry. This settlement was just getting started when the Revolution erupted. They got word that the British, under General Burgoyne, was marching down the Hudson towards Lake Champlain. The British thought if they could divide the northern and southern colonies they could win the war. You know the old saying divide and conquer. Anyway this was most alarming news for the residents of Poultry, and concerned for the safety of their families, they moved the women and children to sanctuary in various towns in Massachusetts, while the men of Poultry decided to join the fight against the Red Coats."

Frederick Weed spoke up and said, "We surely gave those redcoats a good whipping at Saratoga. I believe that's what turned the tide of the war in our favor."

"Yeap," said Charlie, "The Vermont boys were a big factor in turning the tide, and General George sending Morgan up with about three hundred of his finest sharpshooters certainly was a big factor in winning the battle. You know, Morgan's men with those long barreled muskets of theirs, could shoot a hole through a horse's ear at 200 yards."

"My Granddad, Cyrus, was a veteran of the French and

ARNOLD AT SARATOGA
Picture source Wikipedia

Indian War and served on the Committee of Safety for Western Massachusetts. I do believe that my grand dad and all of his sixteen brothers fought in the Revolutionary War together with my dad and a couple of my uncles."

"Granddad Cryus," continued Charley, "was a private under Captain Zenas Wheeler's in Colonel John Ashley's Regiment. He re-enlisted in July of 1777, and served 39 days with an outfit that marched to Fort Edward in response to an alarm. After Burgoyne's surrender at Saratoga, in October of 1777, most of the original settlers of Poultney moved back. Cyrus re-enlisted once again in October of 1880, for six days in Captain Adam Kasson's Company when this unit marched north on an order issued by General Fellows."

Granddad's first wife died when she was young, and he married a second time to Grandma Lois. I never did know her maiden name. My dad Rueben was the oldest of ten."

My daddy, Rueben, was born in New Marlborough in 1753. He was just sixteen when he enlisted in the Revolution, being assigned to William Walker, Superintendent; Captain Kasson's Company, Colonel Ashley's Berkshire Regiment. My father at the time of his enlistment was 5'7" in height, with brown hair. Later, Rueben served under Captain Jeremiah Hickok's Co., Col Elisha Porter's Regiment, commanded by Lt. Col. Sears in the latter part of 1781 for a couple of months. Reuben moved with his family either during the war or shortly after to Poultney, Vermont. In 1800, Reuben moved to Caroga, New York. Here he married Lois. I was second oldest of ten children. Dad died on February 16, 1834, and is buried at Bush Cemetery in Caroga, New York.

"I was born in Poultney, Vt., on January 9, 1794, moved to Caroga Lake with the old man when I was just a kid. Here I met and married sweet Betsy and we got hitched in July of 1820. In the fall of 1839, Betsy and I moved the family here and lived in the Old Pine School House for about a year before buying this land here in Spring Run."

'Well, boys," Charles said to Erasmus and Frederick, "THAT'S THE BROOKINS'S STORY." With that being said, it was getting late, and the visit broke up, and Erasmus and Frederick departed for home.

Charles died on July 29, 1844, at the age of 50. Betsy lived on for another seventeen years, living at the homestead with her children: George, James, Mary, Sally Ann, Silas, Elijah, Harriet and Lucy. Charles and Betsy are buried in the Mt. Zion Cemetery.

Sally Ann, a daughter, married Jacob Ovell and they settled on Mt. Zion Road. Jacob and Sally had nine children.

Elijah Linsley Brookins was born in Caroga Lake, New York on January 8, 1836. He came to Caledonia with has parents when he was about a year old. He enlisted to serve in the Civil War on July 17, 1861, and was assigned to Company G, Forty-second Regiment, P.R.V.C., serving until the close of the war and participated in many battles. He was wounded in the right arm by a ball, and was honorably discharged June 28, 1865. His regiment was known as the old "Bucktails" regiment, which took part in nearly every battle fought by the Army of the Potomac, from Drainesville to the surrender of Lee at Appomattox Courthouse. He returned to his home in November 1868, and married Miss Harriet, a daughter of S. R. and Phoebe (Pearsall) Gardner. She died, June 6, 1875, leaving three children: Alice E., Martha J., and Harriet E. On February 13, 1899, he purchased the homestead in Spring Run consisting of 122 ½ acres located on the Dodge Road from the heirs of his parents. Elijah died in 1908, and is buried at the Mt. Zion Cemetery.

The imaginary encounter – the visit between Erasmus Morey, Frederick Weed and Charles Brookins was fabricated to create a vehicle to present the Brookins story. However, several parts of this introduction are true. Various accounts support Erasmus story on attending the funeral of George Washington; and Frederick Weed was a veteran of the Revolution. Richard Geolott did hold a big Fourth of July event in Medix Run, but it was ten years earlier in 1826, and Charles Brookins did reside in Spring Run.

The Brookins' story as presented through Charles Brookins is based not only on family history, but also on numerous records in the archives of American History. The Brookin's story as presented here establishes a direct line of ancestry from John, the first Brookins in this line to set foot on North American soil to Elijah, a wounded veteran of the Civil War.

The vast majority of American historians agree that the battle of Saratoga was the turning point of the Revolutionary War – a war that gave birth to freedom in a land we know today as United States of America. Most of Philip and Sara Brookin's seventeen sons, if not all of them, fought in the battle of Saratoga, some along with their sons.

When we proudly celebrate our country's birthday on the fourth of July, one knowing the Brookin's family history, might imagine on this glorious day that peering down through the clouds from Heaven above, a group of Brookins with reverence in their hearts and twinkles in their eyes, saying, "WE WERE THERE!"

THE END

History of McKean, Elk, Cameron and Potter Counties, Penna. - Beers
History of the Bucktails – Thomson – Rauch   Morningside
A Brief Sketch of the Brookins Family by Homer De Wilton Brookins – 1924
National Park Service – Saratoga National Historical Park
Wikipedia – The free encyclopedia

THE BLISS FAMILY

The Hymn Singer

Philip Paul Bliss was a lad of 10 years old when he left his family and home on the Bennett's Branch. His sister recalls the day when young Philip left, carrying all his clothes wrapped in a handkerchief; that he never looked back as he walked down the lane leading away from his homestead. Philip, during his short life span of 38 years, would become one of the most distinguished singing evangelists and

Philip Paul Bliss

composers of the century. His legacy to mankind is a collection of hymns and music that is without equal and has remained popular to this day. Philip Bliss perished gallantly on the eve of December 29, 1876, in the worst train accident in US history known at that time.

Isaac Bliss and his wife, Lydia Doolitte Bliss, and two daughters Phoebe and Reliance settled in Slab Town sometime between 1830 and 1838. Slab Town was located just a short distance downstream from Force on the banks of the Bennett's Branch, but the town has long since vanished from the landscape leaving only

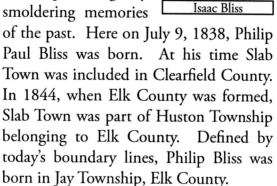

Isaac Bliss

smoldering memories of the past. Here on July 9, 1838, Philip Paul Bliss was born. At his time Slab Town was included in Clearfield County. In 1844, when Elk County was formed, Slab Town was part of Huston Township belonging to Elk County. Defined by today's boundary lines, Philip Bliss was born in Jay Township, Elk County.

PHILIP P. BLISS

The great singing evangelist and gospel song writer was born July 9, 1838, in a log house which stood a little distance from here. He lived and worked on the farm and in nearby lumber camps until the age of 16.

BLISS ROAD SIGN IN
CLEARFIELD COUNTY
HOLLYWOOD, PA.

211

A humble, but happy family, the Blisses lived on the edge of poverty but enjoyed a loving family relationship due to the spiritual inspiration of their father Isaac. Isaac, as described by his daughter, was an extremely devoted religious person with strong family ties, who exhibited a simple child like faith. A man of lovely simplicity, Isaac conducted regular family prayers and spent much of his time reading his bible and singing religious songs. Obviously, Isaac's religious uprightness and example of faith had much to do in molding the character of his son, Philip. When Isaac died on January 1864, Philip made a note in his diary: "Pa Bliss died, the best man I ever knew". Philip had a great affection for his father and dearly loved his memory.

Self-Sufficient at age 10

At the tender age of 10 Philip left home to ease the financial burden on his family. The family was poor, but faithful Christians, rich in family values. Philip, for the next five years of his life, from the age of eleven to sixteen, provided for his own existence, first on a farm, then as an assistant cook in a lumber camp on Pine Creek, in 1853, and later he cut logs in a sawmill in Covington , while attending school when time afforded him the opportunity.

LYDIA DOOLITTLE BLISS

Lydia Doolitte Bliss

When Philip was 17, he worked as a farm hand in Almond, New York, for Mr. O. F. Young for $13 a month, average pay for a farm hand in the 1850's. Mr. Young was a successful farmer, respected in the community, and a member of the Presbyterian Church and local school board. The Youngs were a devout Christian family who loved to sing. Philip, who shared these same values and interests, was invited to make the Young house his home. Shortly after moving in with Youngs, Philip, concerned for the welfare of his younger sister, arranged for her to join the Young family. In 1856, Philip worked on the farm during the summer months, and acquired sufficient education to teach school during the winter months.

LUCY YOUNG BLISS

Lucy Young Bliss

The following year Philip met J.G. Tower, a noted hymn writer, and that winter attended Mr. Tower's singing school where he received his first professional instruction in music. In the following year on June 1, 1859, in Wysocks, New York, Philip, in the company of Ma & Pa Bliss, married Lucy J. Young, the daughter of Mr. O.F. Young.

This was a union made in heaven; their contrasting personalities wholly and completely complemented each other. Some ten year later, Philip would write in his diary (in part): "Truly we have much to be thankful for. My dear wife, my greatest earthly treasure, joins in the opinion that we are and ever have been highly favored of heaven; that we find our greatest enjoyment in each other's society when striving to make each other happy, and our highest aim is to be useful to ourselves and others, and to glorify God that we may enjoy Him forever."

The Sock Funds the Schooling

The following year, Philip found himself in a very upsetting situation. He desperately wanted to attend the Normal Academy of Music at Genesee, N.Y., but lacked the $30 dollars tuition needed to attend. He worried that his entire future had come to an end. His grandmother-in-law, learning of his heartbreaking dilemma, and knowing of his passion for music and need for professional instruction, financed Philip's tuition with coins she had been saving over the years in an old sock for a special occasion. In the winter of 1860, Philip Bliss was recognized by the Music Academy as an outstanding student with considerable talent, and he immediately embarked on his career of teaching music and composing songs. Philip would again attend the Academy in 1861&63 while earning a regular income from teaching music. In the latter sessions, Philip was given special attention and private voice lessons as a result of his recognized talents and inspired drive to learn in his first session.

The Hymnist- Composer

Philip made the acquaintance, probably at the Academy of Music, of hymnist George Root, whose brother W.F. Root, represented the well known music firm in Chicago by the name of Root & Cody. Philip and W.F. carried on a relationship of correspondence, and on one occasion, Philip exchanged a song he wrote entitled "Lora Vale," for a flute. The song became popular and sold several thousand copies. W.F. Root, impressed with Philip as a special person with a talent for song writing, invited him to come to Chicago. Here in Chicago, Philip entered into an agreement to go on tour singing, conducting musical conventions, and promoting music for Root & Cody in the northwestern states and Canada.

Between 1864 and 1876 Philip wrote over eighty songs. These songs included such greats hymns as "Hold the Fort", which was inspired by a message signaled during the civil war by General William T. Sherman; "Almost Persuaded", "Dare to be a Daniel", "Only in Armor Bearer", "Rescue the Perishing", "Pull for the Shore", and "Hallelujah! Tis done!"

During Philip's song writing years, he met the well known evangelist George L. Moody. The two developed an intimate friendship. Moody was overwhelmed by the great power Philip's beautiful and wide ranging baritone had over his audiences. At Moody's encouragement in 1874, Philip gave up all other work to devote his full time and energy to the ministry of gospel music and evangelistic efforts. As a singing evangelist Philip would spend the balance of his short life touring the country conducting and participating in revival meetings and tending to God's work. As a result of these tours, Philip Bliss, would become a national celebrity.

I Know Not The Hour

On the eve of December 29th, 1876, a frigid gale blasted snow at more than 40 miles an hour, faster than the passenger train in which the Blisses traveled, and blew drifts higher than 6 feet on top of the already 3 foot snow fall. It was frigid; twenty degrees or more below zero. In the warm, snug comfort of the heated passenger cars, Philip Bliss and his wife, who had previously been scheduled on an earlier train but due to engine problems rode this train instead, took their last train ride on earth together. That evening after dinner, Philip consoled and lulled his fellow passengers with his last written hymn; a prophecy of what would come on that blackened bitter cold night of fate. "I know Not The Hour" was sung in a deep baritone voice. All were comforted. The ladies and children prepared for bed. The men enjoyed their last smoke or game of cards.

Outside the frosty, snow covered windows lay darkness. The train was two hours late. Finally the whistle blew for the arrival at Ashtabula and the crossing of the "experimental" and controversial bridge built 12 years earlier. The bridge crossed a chasm 70 feet above the Ashtabula River which raged beneath frozen ice floes in depths too dark to see. The HOUR was here. It was now. The greatest and most horrific train accident in the history of the country was happening this very moment. The first engine barely made it across the chasm. The second, engine which held the remaining cars, hung on precariously and then gave way to the frozen depths of the chasm.

The passenger cars tumbled one by one into the frozen abyss, soon to be engulfed in flames of resurrection into the infamy of railroad history and tragedy. Philip Bliss could have survived this most tragic event but he chose to try to rescue his wife who was trapped. His valiant attempt to rescue his dearest one was to no avail. The sky above glowed orange from the inferno below. It was the final encore to "I Know Not the Hour". Philip and Lucy were quickly devoured in the flames at the depth of the gorge.

Atop the hillside of Chestnut Grove Cemetery in Ashtabula, a 35 foot obelisk pointing heavenward memorializes the approximately 200 dead. The Bliss bodies, along with many others, were interred with the unrecognizable charred remains of their fellow travelers of that fateful night.

Bliss's trunk had been checked through to Chicago, and in it, surviving its author, was the last song he wrote, wedding to music the works of Mary G. Brainard., which here seems so fitting:

"I know not what awaits me,
God kindly veils my eyes,
And o'er each step of my onward way
He makes new scenes to rise;
And ev'ry joy He sends me comes
A sweet and glad surprise.
So on I go, not knowing, I would not if I might;
I'd rather walk in the dark with God
Than go alone in the light;
I'd rather walk by faith with Him
Than go alone by sight."

One having a belief in God, and a wild imagination, can only wonder if Jesus Himself didn't greet Philip and Lucy at the pearly gates, with a chorus of angels singing "Hold the Fort"!

THE END

Wesley S. Griswold, Train Wreck!
Biblebelievers. Com/Bliss
The Ashtabula Train Disaster of 1876
Michigan Pioneer and Historical Society
History of McKean, Elk, Cameron and Potter Counties – Beers.

		DATE DUE	

THE LIBRARY STORE   #47-0120

Printed in the United States
218324BV00001B/3/P